NOCTURNAL CREATURES

Robert P. Ottone

Sobelo Books

CONTENTS

ACKNOWLEDGMENTS

I'd like to thank my wife for putting up with my cryptid obsession. It's really quite ridiculous how much I love imagining nocturnal nightmares lurking around every corner, down every lonely street and in every thicket of wood I come across. Thanks, babe!

I'd like to also thank my mom and dad for nurturing a lifelong love of creatures, monsters and more. Without them, I probably wouldn't know what Bigfoot is, let alone more obscure things like the Dover Demon, Mothman or the Jersey Devil. Thanks for getting me weird books and magazines as a kid and fostering a love of things that go bump in the night.

Last but not least, all the readers. I don't ever want to undersell how important you all are to us. You're willing to pay hard-earned money for a scrappy, brutal horror book like this one? That's awesome. If I ever meet you, or you see me out somewhere, whether I'm with Bigfoot or not, say hi. You have my eternal gratitude.

Now, let's see what's lurking in those woods and mountains.

CHAPTER ONE

Cassie lay on her brother Morgan's bed listening to REM's *Out of Time* on his boom box. It was one of the more recent albums he picked up before shipping out for the Marines three months earlier. She was sure not to disturb the blankets or the sheets on the bed and she was always careful about placing his cassettes back in their correct spaces on his enormous tape cabinet. Cassie hadn't taken an exact count of the tapes, but there must have been a thousand.

Cassie felt Morgan would like to come home and see everything in exactly the same place as he left it so any time she borrowed a t-shirt, hockey jersey, flannel or hoodie, she was exceedingly careful to not get it dirty. Upon finishing the school day, she would carefully hang the borrowed article exactly where she found it in the closet. She never bothered with the jeans in the middle dresser drawer or the socks and boxers in the top drawer. She had made the mistake of opening the bottom drawer only once, and the women on the covers of Morgan's "secret stash" were enough to keep Cassie away from that particular drawer for the rest of her life.

Cassie was looking for her brother's old ChatBoy cassette recorder. Before he left, Morgan recorded a full ninety-minute tape of his favorite songs, interspersed with stories and anecdotes for her. The last time she listened to it, she left it somewhere in Morgan's old room but couldn't figure out exactly where. Eventually, she found it under the bed with dust balls and other junk like her brother's old catcher's mitt, Cassie's duffel bag from when she was on the track team and other junk.

Cassie loved listening to Morgan's stories, like Cassie's first attempt at cutting her own hair and how she spent that summer wearing ski caps and hoodies to hide the fact that her hair had to be trimmed insanely short so it would grow back evenly. That's around the time she got comfy wearing Morgan's Yankee cap nearly every day. Once he shipped out, it rarely left her head. Cassie laughed at all the same points on the tape: the forking of Old Man Fanning's lawn, schlocking Mike Addeo with fifty cent shakes from McDonald's, pulling a lawn job on Morgan's ex-girlfriend's front lawn. Reckless, silly stuff that never failed to make Cassie laugh when she heard Morgan tell the story. Sometimes he'd just burp or say a weird string of words (his favorite was "subterranean nuclear silo") or a dirty limerick from the joke book Cassie got him the Christmas before he shipped out.

The boom box automatically flipped to the second side and Cassie smiled in the fading beam of light coming over her family's orchard. REM was one of her favorites. Morgan's, too. He started getting into harder stuff before he enlisted. Bands like Pearl Jam, Nine Inch Nails, The Smashing Pumpkins and more. Cassie liked them, but she enjoyed more mellow stuff like The Violent Femmes, Siouxsie & The Banshees, and Blur. She figured the hard stuff might grow on her. Until then, she liked bopping along with the music he shared with her.

She rose from the bed and took off her brother's New York Yankees hoodie, hanging it exactly where she found it that morning before school. She brushed her long hair from her face and heard her mother's voice in her head. *Cassandra, we need to cut that hair. It's too long for the summer.* Even though it was May, Cassie couldn't shake the cold from her bones and was glad to keep her long hair. Upstate New York had seen an unseasonably chilly spring, especially in the foothills along the western expanse of the Dunderberg Mountains where her family's orchard sat, surrounded by thick woods. Summer had yet to warm, and Cassie was wondering if she'd be wearing hoodies and flannels through August. The property stretched to the forest at the base of the mountain, but between the Dunderbergs and the outskirts of the orchard was a guest house Cassie's parents rented to seasonal workers or visiting family. It sat empty since last summer when their previous tenant, a hard worker and friend of the family, moved south to Florida to take care of his sick mother.

Cassie stared at the framed family photo on Morgan's desk and the other junk he left behind. The picture was taken on

Christmas Eve two years ago when Cassie was eleven and featured both Morgan and Cassie staring into the camera, faking disinterest in order to look *cool* (her brother's word). If it wasn't for the fact that Cassie emulated her brother in nearly every way, it would be impossible to guess they were related.

Morgan looked so much like their mom, Krystal. He had the same delicate features, narrow nose and dirty blond hair. Cassie was almost the spitting image of their dad, Bernardo. Nardo to those close to him. Black hair. Thick, dark eyebrows that Cassie wrestled into submission daily. Olive complexion. Cassie always loved when her dad would have a little too much wine and start telling the story of when he met her mom. After he came to America from Naples in 1975, he met Krystal at a carnival outside of the Hollow. To hear Krystal tell it, she swooned at the accent first, then swooned at how driven he was to make a life for himself in America. "A whirlwind romance to the most beautiful woman I ever met," Nardo would say, his accent rising to the surface the more he drank. The two got married in '76, Morgan came along about six months later and the pair saved every penny they could scrape together to buy the orchard. Bernardo had been working there since he arrived from the old country, and he loved the area. He would joke that the soil had become a part of him. He loved the hard work of growing the delicious fruit their orchard was known for.

Cassie gazed out the window overlooking one hundred acres of apples and peaches. She hoped Morgan would be back in time for the harvest in late August. Not just to help with picking the fruit, but also just because she missed him. Time without Morgan was wasted. He never failed to hug her before school and was ready to help with her homework when she returned. Even between taking classes at the community college, working a part-time job at the local sporting goods store and helping around the orchard, Morgan made time for Cassie and she missed that.

"Cassandra, homework!" her mom called from downstairs.

Cassie rolled her eyes, then turned and headed to the bedroom door. She took one last look around and sighed.

"See you later," she said, leaving the room.

As Cassie entered the living room, she spotted her dad sitting at the kitchen table. There were papers scattered all over the place and an accordion folder on the floor beside his nervously tapping foot.

"Hey *Cucciola*," Bernardo said, using his favorite Italian pet name for Cassie. When Cassie first asked her mom what the word meant, she learned it was a catch-all of sorts for *baby critter* or *little pet* and Cassie smiled when he said it. After years of hearing the word, Cassie started feeling awkward when he used it. "You hit the books yet?"

Cassie shook her head. "I don't have a lot."

"Better get to it!" her mom's voice called from the pantry. "Otherwise, no movies this weekend."

"Krys, she'll get it done," Bernardo said. "She always does. Right, *Cucciola*?"

Cassie thought of saying something to her dad. Maybe asking him to dial back on the *Cucciola* stuff, but never did. Sure, the term embarrassed her, but it was his little nickname, and she knew he meant it with love. Cassie wasn't fully in the rebellious youth phase of her teens, but she could feel it lurking around the corner.

"Yeah," Cassie nodded. She looked over the papers. None of them made sense to her. "What is all this stuff? Homework?"

"Very funny, *Cucciola*," Bernardo said with a chuckle. "Just some papers for work. Nothing to worry about."

Cassie's eyes focused on a repeated phrase stamped on the papers in red lettering: Final Notice

"Cassandra Michelle Albero, I am *not* kidding." Krystal popped her head out of the pantry. "If you don't get that homework done before dinner, I swear to God."

Bernardo and Cassie shared an eye roll and Cassie grabbed her backpack from the kitchen counter and headed to the living room. She unpacked her notebook and began working on the short answer questions for English. A series of questions about *The Outsiders*. Cassie found herself tearing up in class as they finished it and ducked into the bathroom to dry her eyes, desperate to not be known as a wimp who cried over the ending of some stupid book. Still, knowing how Johnny suffered all through the book and reading how that affected Dallas Winston ... it was all too much for Cassie. And forget about watching the movie. Those beautiful boys and their troubles. Cassie found herself both in love and heartbroken all at the same time.

"How's it looking?" Krystal asked Bernardo as she placed dinner supplies on the counter.

Bernardo tried to keep his voice low, but Cassie's determined ears still made out the words. "Gonna' be tight if we don't have a good harvest."

"We have that prospective tenant coming this weekend, so that'll help, right?" Krystal asked, concern causing her voice to crack.

"It'll help for sure. We're going to be fine. I didn't think a cold spring could hurt us so much."

Krystal rubbed his shoulders. After a moment, she leaned down and kissed Bernardo's forehead. "I better get dinner started, 'Nardo."

As she started toward the counter, Bernardo slapped her butt and Cassie made a face. "Ew, Dad!"

Bernardo and Krystal laughed as Cassie shrunk into the couch in embarrassment.

CHAPTER TWO

Cassie sat on the steps of the guest house with Bernardo. They were sharing a Pepsi. The weekend came quickly and even though she had some schoolwork to finish, she was far more interested in meeting the folks who'd be living in the guest house than anything related to algebra or whatever nonsense her math teacher was throwing at her. She passed the bottle to her dad and he took a sip. Krystal emerged from the front door and tucked the guest house keys in her jeans pocket.

A distant sound came from over Cassie's shoulder. Almost like fireworks, but further away and only twice, echoing in the Dunderbergs. She looked towards the mountains and saw the tiniest cloud of smoke emerge from the forest before it vanished in the air.

"They're blowing stuff up again," Cassie said. "What if one of those bombs goes off and blows up more than the old mines?"

Bernardo chuckled. "That can't happen. They don't use too much explosive. Just *enough*. Those mines are dangerous. The cave system goes deep. Me and your mama used to go there when we first started dating. She'd get scared and want to turn around the second we'd step into the caves."

Cassie furrowed her brow at her dad. "Mom always said *you* were the one who got scared. You'd curse in Italian and the next thing she knew, you'd be running back the way you came."

Bernardo laughed. He handed the Pepsi back to Cassie and she took a sip. "Your mama's tough, that's for sure. Even with a flashlight, those caves are dark. Back home, in the Dolomite Mountains, there were fairies and sprites that lived in the caves."

"Aww, dad, stop it ..." Cassie groaned.

"I'm serious, *Cucciola*," Bernardo said. He smiled. "I guess you're too old for these silly stories, huh?"

Cassie shrugged. "I still love them. I just know better than to believe in monsters in the mountains and the woods and stuff. I'm a cool kid."

"That is for certain, little one. That is for certain." He wrapped an arm around her. "Not too cool to hug your old man, though, so that's good."

She smiled up at Bernardo. Cassie appreciated how fanciful he could be and remembered nearly word for word the stories and myths he told her of the old country. She hoped to one day travel with him there and see the places she only knew from his stories and the Polaroids he kept in a shoebox under the coffee table. Whenever they had guests, he'd pop the top off the box and show visitors pictures of the Italian coast, the mountains, the wineries, and orchards he worked on as a young man. Bernardo was proud of his country, proud of his heritage, and he wanted his children to be the same way.

"Oh! I forgot to check the storage under the stairs!" Krystal said, ducking back into the house. Cassie's mom was meticulous with stuff like this. She kept a clean house, sure, but Cassie and Bernardo helped. When it came to the guest house, because Krystal's passion was in real estate, she wanted to present the guest house as an oasis. It had to smell good. Look good. Every inch clean.

The guest house was about three hundred yards from the main home and Cassie thought about how she and Morgan used to race from their porch to the guest house, sprinting at top speed. Morgan would make it there in less than a minute and a half. Cassie, usually around two. Typically, the guest house was about a four-minute walk through the orchard, longer if Cassie took one of the many rows that stretched the length of the orchard proper. She preferred cutting through the trees, which could sometimes be a problem if she disturbed the fruit, but as she got older, she grew more careful.

Krystal returned to the porch, making a note on the listing documents.

"Everything good, Mama?" Bernardo asked.

"Place is spotless. Furniture's in good shape," Krystal said, looking over the front porch of the guest house. "The upstairs deck could use a good stainin', but I don't think anyone'd mind."

The guest house was a simple two-story Victorian painted light gray with burgundy shutters. A large root cellar allowed for extra storage of whatever the tenant may need, and the ancient cellar door was a home repair Bernardo kept neglecting. The wood doors were still in good shape, but Bernardo would remark to Cassie, during each repair, that they should update them. "Some nice metal ones, you know?" he'd say.

"Someday, little one, you can move in here," Bernardo said, putting his arm around Cassie. "We can make it nicer for you while you go to college."

"Cool," Cassie said, shrugging. She hadn't thought about college. She hadn't thought about much of anything other than Morgan coming home. Going to college was important to her parents. Her mom didn't go to college, and instead worked in real estate part-time while running the orchard's tiny store. "What are these people's names?"

"It's a mother and her son. Let me check," Krystal said, fishing for some paperwork in her back pocket. She unfolded it and looked it over quickly. "Azura and Darwin Pineda. They're from El Salvador but have been renting in Lakeside the past two years."

"Where is El Salvador? Salvador who? Dali?" Bernardo joked, finishing the Pepsi. "Oh, *Cucciola*, mi dispiace."

"It's okay," Cassie said, taking the empty bottle from her dad. "El Salvador is in Central America, I think."

Bernardo grinned proudly. "You're so smart, Cassandra. You know everything." He put an arm around her and gave her a squeeze.

"It's just geography, Dad. Jeez."

Krystal laughed and tucked the paperwork away as a sedan pulled down the side driveway. Their property had two entrances to the main road, one on the side for whoever was living in the guest house and the main entrance Cassie's family shared with visitors to the orchard. That entrance led to a large open dirt parking area, which was always packed come fall with families and couples drawn to upstate New York for weekends of apple and peach picking and posing in the small field where Krystal grew pumpkins. She loved watching little kids toddle around the pumpkin patch, looking for the perfect gourd to turn into the perfect jack-o'-lantern.

The sedan rolled to a stop in the driveway and Krystal stepped off the porch, waving. She walked over to the car and waved again as who could only be Azura opened the driver-side door. Cassie had never met the woman before and didn't know what to expect, but the girl's eyes went wide as she watched the raven-haired woman stepped out of the car.

"Nice to meet you," Krystal began, shaking the woman's hand. Azura's black jeans matched her black t-shirt. The words *Yolocamba Ita* stretched across the chest. Her dark hair was pulled back in a messy bun and she wore a pair of cheap dollar store sunglasses, black lenses with neon pink frames. Immediately, Cassie thought she looked cool.

"You must be Krystal," Azura said. When she smiled, Cassie thought she might be older than she first appeared, her dark skin stretching and revealing wrinkles Cassie didn't notice upon first glance. "I hope our application is all good?"

"Oh, most definitely," Krystal said. "I was just taking a look around inside; I think you and your son will be happy. Hopefully!"

The two women shared a laugh. Cassie and Bernardo rolled their eyes. The passenger door opened and a young boy stepped out. He was tall. Lanky is perhaps a better term, with the faintest hint of a mustache growing on his upper lip. Cassie figured he was her age, possibly a little older. Cassie watched as his bushy hair caught the wind and she stared at the boy a moment, before turning quickly so he wouldn't think she was a creep.

"And you're Darwin! Nice to meet you, too!" Krystal beamed.

"Hi," he said, shaking her hand. He had on a gray t-shirt and a simple pair of blue jeans, with a flannel tied around his waist. "Nice to meet you."

Darwin walked over and shook Bernardo's hand. He then extended his hand to Cassie, but before she could take it, a light tinkling caught her attention and she turned toward the noise. A trio of tiny rocks rolled down the roof of the guest house before smacking to the ground and kicking up a bit of dust.

Cassie looked around, trying to figure out where the rocks had come from. From the nearby forest, she saw the faintest hint of movement as the trees swayed in the wind.

"That's weird," the boy said. "Hi, I'm Darwin."

Cassie shook his hand. "Cassie."

He smiled awkwardly, his lips tightening, pressing together in a way that made them look like they may pop off his face, then tucked his hands in his pockets. Cassie figured he was fifteen at most.

"Don't be *awkward*," Azura said with a smirk, nudging Darwin. "Shall we go inside?"

Krystal led them up the steps to the front door while Bernardo and Cassie remained in the driveway, watching the forest. Bernardo walked over to the rocks, knelt down, and picked them up, examining them closely. He tossed one to Cassie. "What's that look like to you?"

"A rock," Cassie said, smiling.

"Very funny, smartass. What *kind*?"

She examined the rock closely. Segments of the rock glittered faintly in the light. "This looks like quartz."

"Do we dig up much quartz around here?" Bernardo asked, standing up and stretching his back. He held the other two rocks in his hands, about the size of ping-pong balls.

"Closer to the river up the mountain. Before it empties into one of the basins?"

Bernardo nodded. "How does a rock from one of the rivers up the mountain end up rolling down the roof of our guest house?"

Cassie furrowed her brow. "It doesn't."

Bernardo nodded. "Good girl. Go inside and help your mama, *Cucciola*."

"What about you?"

Bernardo stared at the woods. "I'm gonna' go have a look in the woods. I'll be back before you're all done."

With that, Bernardo walked toward the verdant darkness of the thicket of aspen, ash, and birch trees that framed the orchard. Cassie felt a pang of anxiety tear through her stomach as he disappeared, the woods devouring his form.

🦍 🦍 🦍

Cassie entered the guest house and looked around. She loved the fireplace along the far wall and remembered their former tenant using it often. Cassie could almost smell the wood burning, the smoke puffing from the chimney. She stepped over the thick beams of light coming in from the windows of the living room and looked out the window toward the woods, hoping to see her dad re-emerge. Instead, she only saw the trees swaying lazily in the breeze.

"I thought it'd be smaller," Darwin said behind her. She turned with a start and sighed.

"What? The house?"

He nodded. "Yeah, our last place was tiny compared to this. Not just the house. This whole orchard. It's pretty."

"You should see it when all the *citiots* are here. You won't think it's so pretty, then."

"What does that mean? *Citiots*?" Darwin asked.

"Oh, it's a combo of 'city' and 'idiot.' All the people from Manhattan and the metro part of New York that come up here to pick their own pumpkins, apples and peaches and stuff," Cassie explained. "They're the worst. You'll see."

"I've never been to New York City before." He pulled an old, dirty New York Yankees baseball cap out of his back pocket and put it on. "I really want to go to Yankee Stadium, though."

"That's in the Bronx. Not quite Manhattan," Cassie said with a smile.

"You've been there?"

"Yeah, my dad's taken me to a few games. I used to go with my brother, too."

Darwin nodded and smiled. Cassie thought he was almost too excited, like a puppy. "Where is your brother?"

"He's in Iraq. In the war."

"Oh wow. He's brave. Like my papa."

Darwin pulled on a thin, black piece of leather around his neck. Dangling in the light of the living room on a thin piece of wood were the letters *FMLN* in red with a star over the F. The wood was carved into a shield-like shape, almost like a coat of arms. Two machine guns crisscrossed over the letters, and the bottom was framed with an intricate image of green laurel.

"What's that?" Cassie asked, leaning in for a better look. They weren't more than a foot apart now.

"Freedom fighters in my country. This was my papa's."

"Can I see it?"

Darwin nodded and she reached out, holding the pendant in her hand. It was cool to the touch and light, almost shiny, as though varnished. "What happened to your dad?"

Slowly, Darwin tucked the necklace back into his shirt. "He was taken by the police after a battle. I don't know what happened to him."

Cassie stared at the boy. There was hurt in his eyes, but he held it back.

"I'm so sorry."

Darwin nodded. "I was very little. My mama was with him when they took him, but she got away. He gave her this to give to me as the police came and got him."

"Your mom was a freedom fighter, too?"

Another nod. "She was a mechanic back home. Fixed up the cars, trucks and machinery my dad and his friends were using. She can fix anything."

Cassie smiled. "That's really cool. Really badass."

"She *is* really badass, that's a good way to put it," Darwin said, smiling.

They stood there in awkward silence for a minute.

"You wanna' see something cool?" Cassie asked, finally breaking the silence.

"Yes, please."

With that, she took Darwin's hand and led him out the front door.

Cassie ran through the orchard, Darwin close behind. Tree branches whipped her sides as they sprinted until, finally, they came to a clearing. Twenty feet of grass lay between the two kids and a steep drop. The drop led to a pit of sorts, littered with broken glass, bits and pieces of metal machinery, rubber tires, and more. Cassie stepped to the edge and looked down. She huffed to catch her breath as she stared down at the mix of broken debris at the bottom.

She turned toward Darwin. "Come here."

"That looks steep. I don't think I should."

"Don't be a wimp. Come here," Cassie repeated. "I promise it's not as far down as it looks. Eight feet at most?"

The pit was only about nine feet wide and could be passed easily in certain sections where the debris inside wasn't too high. Even in the handful of sections where there was no debris, there were thick pieces of rock and stone, along with a bedding of sand and even patches of colorful wildflowers.

Slowly, Darwin stepped to the edge of the pit beside her. He looked to the left and right and saw that the pit stretched along the eastern perimeter of the orchard. "What is this?"

Cassie shrugged. "I think the people who owned the orchard before my dad bought it used to just dump their broken equipment in this pit. So, me and my brother used to come here and throw soda bottles and other crap in there to watch it explode into a million pieces. My bro and I call it The Pit."

Darwin smiled. "That's pretty cool."

"Toldja."

"Is the whole pit like this?"

"Just this part down to like, right before my house down there," Cassie said excitedly, pointing. "Old tractor pieces. Pipes. Morgan, he's my brother. He thinks the people who started the orchard way back in the day built this as a kind of drainage runoff or something. We even found horseshoes once, which was pretty cool."

"Horseshoes are to keep bruja away," Darwin said quietly.

"What's a *broo-ha*?"

"It's like a witch. They're not all bad, but you hang a horseshoe over the doorway of your house to keep the bad ones away or something like that."

Cassie nodded. "That's really cool."

"I know lots about witches and ghosts and monsters. I used to read about them when I was little."

Cassie sat down along the ledge, her legs dangling. She looked down at the rainbow of broken glass bottles that mingled with the jagged and rusty pieces of metal. "I used to read about that stuff, too. Well, not really. My brother would read that stuff to me to freak me out before bed. Schmuck."

Darwin laughed. He sat down beside her and carefully let his legs dangle, too. "I didn't bring the book with me when we came here. I wish I did."

"Be cool if it was the same one. Tell me another one."

He smiled. "Sure. You ever hear the story of Barney and Betty Hill?"

Cassie shook her head. She squinted in the sunlight as Darwin started his tale.

Later that night, Bernardo sat in his favorite chair, rolling one of the rocks around in his hand. The family was watching the news, where footage of the Gulf War played on-screen. Planes dropping bombs. Men in camouflage standing in the desert. Iraqi women and children being evacuated.

Cassie turned, expecting to see her dad watching the news. Instead, he simply stared at the rock with a distant look in his eye. Cassie couldn't tell exactly what the look was, because she had never seen it on her dad before. Maybe it was confusion? Worry?

"You okay, Pop?" Cassie asked.

He looked up at her and smiled. His eyes were glassy, as though he hadn't blinked in a while. Cassie couldn't remember seeing him blink once in the time she stared at him. "Of course, *Cucciola*. Everything's good."

Cassie knew better. The last time she saw her dad like this was the morning after Morgan had told the family that he had enlisted. Cassie eventually figured out what the look on her father's face meant.

Bernardo was scared.

🦍 🦍 🦍

That night, as Cassie lay in bed reading, Bernardo came to the door and peeked inside.

"Lights out, little one." He reached for the light.

"Dad," Cassie began. "What did you find in the woods? You never told me."

He flicked the light switch off and was backlit by the hall light. Cassie always hated the outline of a person standing in her doorway. Even as she got older, it still sent a creep up her spine. Instinctively, she tucked herself into her blankets more.

"Just some kids, sweetheart. Nothing to worry about. Kids playing games," he said. "Get some sleep. I love you." There was a hitch in his voice and Cassie knew exactly what that meant. Her dad was lying.

"I love you too, dad. Good night."

Chapter Three

Monday came quickly and Cassie found herself bored in class. She sat with her friends in the lunchroom, made tentative plans to ride bikes that weekend, and just went through her school day, excited to return home and listen to music in Morgan's room.

After she listened to The Ocean Blue's self-titled album start to finish on Morgan's boom box, Cassie found herself behind the wheel of his El Camino. The car was his pride and joy, as beat up as it was. Morgan worked two summers straight to save up for it, putting money down at the garage in town to keep it reserved for him until he could pay it off completely. Krystal kept the keys in her pocketbook, should Cassie get any *bright ideas* as her mom would put it. She'd usually pretend Morgan was driving her to 4th World Comics to pick up Superman comics or to Taco Bell for a Meximelt. Sometimes she'd bring the ChatBoy with her and play it, imagining Morgan was right there beside her, telling her the jokes and stories live.

Piercing the sounds of Ned's Atomic Dustbin on the Chat-Boy, Cassie caught the tail-end of a sharp, staccato *whoop* noise in the distance. She clicked the tape recorder off and listened. *Whoop–whoop–whoop* erupted from the woods and the mountains behind. Cassie hadn't heard a sound like that before, or had never noticed it so clearly. She sat behind the wheel of the El Camino and continued listening, noticing the unusual lack of sound in the area. No bugs buzzing around. No birds chirping. Absolutely nothing. She sat in perfect silence for a while longer before climbing out of the El Camino and trying to figure out what else she could do with what was left of her afternoon.

Eventually, Cassie found herself walking along the long dirt driveway toward the road. She paused, thinking of the sound from the woods, and ducked into the orchard itself, slipping over to the guest house's driveway and snuck a peek at Azura and Darwin as they were carrying large cardboard boxes, each labeled in black marker with a different room of the guest house. There was a medium-sized U-Haul parked in the driveway. Darwin carried a box that read "LIBROS" in thick black lettering. He placed it down on the porch to catch his breath as Azura walked by, carrying a box the same size.

Cassie hid behind a thick outcropping of bushes that lined the guest house property from that section of the orchard. Krystal and Bernardo had planted the bushes here to give their tenants a semblance of privacy and separation during the busy months on the orchard. The bushes were thick, but one could still see through once their eyes adjusted.

"Come on, *hijo*," she said, nudging him with her hip. "Be strong for Mama and carry your books upstairs."

"I know, I know," he said, wiping the sweat from his brow. Cassie watched as he knelt down and carried the box inside.

Sneaking closer, but staying within the rows of the orchard, Cassie tried to get a better look. Darwin re-emerged from the house carrying a cold bottle of Jolt Cola. He twisted the cap and took a sip. As he sighed, he turned and spotted Cassie in the rows of apple trees.

"Hey," he said with a wave.

"Hi."

He looked around nervously. "What're you doing?"

Cassie stepped out from the bushes and nervously adjusted her backpack. She shrugged. "Dunno. Thought I'd see if you guys were getting along okay. See how moving was going."

"It's good. Your mom was over earlier. She helped us with the beds and the heavy furniture."

"Bitchin'," Cassie said. "You guys have more to move in?"

Azura emerged from the house. "Oh, hi Cassie. How was school?"

"Good. Boring. Do you need some help?"

Azura smiled. "There's not much left to do, *querida*, but if you wouldn't mind helping Darwin put the dishes and pots away, that'd be awful nice. I was going to hang some photos and stuff."

Cassie nodded and walked over. Following Azura inside, she looked around. The guest house looked more like a home with Azura and Darwin's stuff in various stages of set-up. There were a couple photos on the wall, including one of a handsome thick-bearded man carrying a machine gun and smoking a cigarette. He wore a green bandana and smiled for the camera; his eyes closed.

"Is this your dad?" Cassie asked.

"Yeah," Darwin said. He pointed at the necklace around his dad's neck.

"He looks so cool."

"*Muy chido*. The *coolest*," Azura said. She placed a hand on the framed photo. "I took this of him when his platoon got back from a fight. They didn't lose anyone and wanted to celebrate, so I took pictures of him and his friends. This one was my favorite."

"I can see why," Cassie said. "Did you fight in the war, too?"

"Everybody fought. Whether they did with weapons or not. All our people fought."

Cassie didn't quite understand what Azura meant. The woman stared at the picture of her husband a moment before sighing and walking over to a large opened box of photos. Cassie couldn't help but feel sad for her, even if she didn't understand what Azura was feeling.

"Come on," Darwin said, walking toward the kitchen. It was around the corner from the front living room, further back, with the stairs and a small hallway separating them from the kitchen and downstairs bathroom. Once in the kitchen, Cassie and Darwin set about putting the plates and utensils away.

Later, Cassie and Darwin sat on the front porch drinking Jolt Colas. Azura came out carrying a small plate of carrots, Oreos, and celery.

"What does 'querida' mean?"

"Ummm," Darwin began. "How to say ... it's like a nice thing, like saying 'sweetheart' or 'darling.'"

Cassie tried to hide her smile, ducking her head and letting her hair fall over her face. She looked over the plate of snacks.

"This is a weird mix of things, I know. I need to go food shopping tomorrow," Azura said, placing the plate between Darwin and Cassie.

"These are three of my favorite things," Cassie said, crunching into a carrot.

Darwin grabbed an Oreo, opened it, and licked the cream from within before placing the cookie part back together and taking a bite.

"That's weird," Cassie said, looking up at Azura. "That's how he eats them?"

Azura laughed. "I didn't teach him that, so don't blame me. You two stay out of trouble. I'm gonna' hang some pictures upstairs," she said, heading inside. "Hey Cassie. Thanks for your help, sweetie. Thank your mama again for us."

Cassie smiled and waved. "No *problemo*, Mrs. Pineda."

Azura cringed. "Eww, no '*Mrs. Pineda*' stuff. Call me Azura."

"Will do ... Azura."

"Much better," the woman said before disappearing up the stairs.

"Your mom is awesome," Cassie said, taking a chunk out of a celery stick. "She doesn't act like my mom. She doesn't act like *any* mom, actually."

Darwin nodded. "Yeah," he said. The boy almost looked a little sad when he said it, but Cassie couldn't figure out why. "Did your dad figure out where those rocks came from?"

"He hasn't said much about it since the other day. We were watching TV later that night and he was weird about it."

"Maybe a witch put a spell on him."

"Shut up, no way," Cassie said. "He still has one of the rocks. I'll ask him tonight." She finished her soda and grabbed an Oreo. "I gotta get goin'."

"Cool. Thank you again for helping us out."

Cassie smiled. "How come you don't go to school?"

He shrugged. "Mom says I don't need to."

"Wish my mom said I didn't need to," Cassie said with a sigh. She started towards the rows of apple and peach trees, wondering how mad her parents would be with her returning home so long after school, but stopped and turned back to the boy. "What're you doing tomorrow?"

"Helping mom with a few cars during the day. Nothing after that. Why?"

"My dad didn't tell me the truth about what he saw in the woods when you guys arrived," she said.

"So?"

"So sew your pants," Cassie said with a sly grin.

"I don't understand," Darwin said, shrugging and sipping his Jolt Cola.

"It's a joke. Anyway, I think we should go into the woods and see for ourselves. My dad said it was kids."

"Then it was probably kids," Darwin said, leaning back on his hands.

"*We're* kids. I've got a pretty good arm and I don't think I could launch a rock from the forest to the roof of the house." She waited a moment. "Could *you* throw a rock that high onto a roof?"

"Maybe," he said, furrowing his brow.

"You could barely carry that box of books. Listen, I'm gonna' go into the woods and take a look around. If you wanna' come with, be at The Pit at like, four o'clock."

Cassie turned and ducked into the orchard.

🦍 🦍 🦍

As Cassie made her way to her house through the rows of fruit trees, she picked up the scent of something foul on the wind. She stopped and looked around, wondering if a skunk was nearby. She had smelled plenty of skunks and while this wasn't exactly the same, it was similar and Cassie worried that at any moment she could be sprayed by one of the little black and white buggers. As quickly as the odor hit her, it dissipated and Cassie continued on her way.

The sun was setting and the sky burned orange. The way the oranges burned away to purple for a moment as day turned to night in the sky above the Dunderberg mountains was her brother's favorite sight. Over time, it became hers, too. She would sit at the edge of the orchard with her brother almost every summer night, watching the sun set.

Sniff. Cassie took a few tentative sniffs of the air, again picking up the foul aroma. It danced around her nostrils, somehow heavier. She looked at the ground, expecting a skunk to be toddling around in the vicinity, but again saw nothing.

"Whatever ..." she said, pulling her t-shirt up over her nose to lessen the scent. Cassie continued through the orchard. She was about halfway to her house, and could see the lights on in the living room and kitchen.

Cassie took a few more steps, eyes on the glowing windows.

Suddenly, she heard a low rumble behind her. She stopped and turned, expecting to see a bear, an angry fox, or even a boar, but instead saw nothing. The smell hung in the air and she looked around, confused. The scent was suffusing, familiar. *I know that stink*, Cassie thought.

She quickened her pace. The sound came again from behind her, but this time, she didn't stop. It grew in volume, and she listened until it faded and died out completely. *What could make a sound like that?* Cassie wondered. As she breached the tree line of the orchard and her family's property, she stopped again and turned around. In the fading daylight gloom, she thought she saw two yellow-red eyes glowing in the distance. Orbs that hung above the apple and peach trees. At least *two feet* above them. Cassie strained her eyes but couldn't make out much more within the dark gloom and the glow that seemed to stare directly back at her. The light from the house reflected in them, and they flickered for an instant. A pang of terror coursed through her body, goosebumps flickering across her flesh when she thought she saw a pair of glowing red eyes in the orchard behind her. *But that would be impossible,* she thought.

The low, tremulous rumble gave way to a deafening bellow. Starting deep, the sound surged in volume. *Ughhhhraaaaaaaa.* Cassie continued to stare, frozen in place. She wanted to run, but her legs refused to cooperate. Cassie was reminded of the air raid drills at school. She and her classmates would have to duck under their desks and wait it out, as the sirens screamed, echoing in the hallways and through each classroom. She hated fire drills, air raid drills, *any* kind of drill. The noise was all-encompassing and rattled her to the core.

The roar tore through her body and shook the very ground she stood on until finally, breaking the spell, she bolted for the front door of the main house, opening the screen door and closing it. She locked it quickly, then closed the heavy wooden front door, locking it as well.

Slowly, she slid to the ground, back to the door, and caught her breath.

Krystal stood at the top of the steps, staring down at her.

"Everything okay, honey?"

Chapter Four

There was no sleep to be had for Cassie. She lay in bed, eyes darting from one window to another, expecting to see eyes staring in at her. Though she was upstairs, her mind raced at the possibility of something enormous just climbing into her window and tearing her to shreds. The safety of her bedroom was violated. She couldn't get the creature's growl out of her mind. She heard it over and over, a low grumble to a roar that reminded her of the time she went to the air show with her dad and brother and the fighter jets zoomed over their heads.

The ferocity of the sound scared her then. The ferocity of whatever was in the orchard scared her now.

She tried telling her mom, but Krystal just thought Cassie was tired. When Cassie told Bernardo, he nodded slowly, as if he understood. He then told her not to worry, got her a glass of water, and told her to sit with him and watch TV.

The entire time on the couch, Cassie had one eye on the window behind her dad. She envisioned whatever was in the orchard bursting through and yanking Bernardo from his chair. She would watch as her dad died screaming, half torn apart by the jagged shards of window left behind in the creature's wake.

Stop it, Cassie thought, trying to push the image from her mind.

Outside, the wind blew through the leaves of the fruit trees. The screech of an owl, somewhere in the distance. The creak of the weathervane on top of the house.

🦍 🦍 🦍

The following morning, Cassie felt the exhaustion of being up nearly the entire night as she showered and got ready for school. She dozed off under the warm spray of water in the bathroom and only shook the sleep away once she heard her mom clanging pots and pans downstairs.

Grabbing a Pop-Tart and running out the door, Cassie walked quickly and, even in the daylight, felt nervous as she strode past the orchard. She took short glances into the trees, worried those two glowing eyes would be staring at her through the foliage. She shuddered at the thought of seeing it in the daylight, imagining wings, tentacles and other nightmarish possibilities.

Cassie caught the bus in time and spent the rest of the day thinking about the eyes in the orchard. When she tried to focus on schoolwork, the eyes were there. The mossy, mildewy smell that reminded her of their basement when it flooded four summers earlier. The roar that sounded so much like a siren. *How could something make that sound?*

In the school library, Cassie searched the shelves for books on wildlife. She found multiple volumes on birds, hunting deer, and more. She flipped through a few books on bears, elk and other creatures, but nothing matched the height of what she saw in the orchard.

In a book by one Dr. Ronald Bimboo, Cassie found a picture of a grizzly bear on its hind legs. Next to it was a picture of Bimboo himself, standing six feet tall. The bear was easily two feet taller, and the caption read *Dr. Bimboo and Shiloh the Grizzly, Yellowstone 1988.*

According to the book, wild grizzly bears no longer existed east of the Great Plains. In another book titled *The Wilds of New York* by "noted outdoorsman and wildlife enthusiast" Mike Davis, she found images of black bears standing on their hind legs. The paragraph preceding the photo read:

"The black bear of North America is largely an omnivore and is, by far, the most abundant across the country. Male and female black bears, when on their hind legs, can be as tall as seven feet and often weigh upwards of 400 lbs. They make their homes traditionally in thick forest, and have a varied and expansive diet."

Cassie furrowed her brow and continued reading. The book, while interesting, didn't offer much to guide her research. While she did come away with an abundance of bear facts, when staring at the close-up photos of the creatures' eyes, none matched what she saw in the darkness of the orchard.

🐻 🐻 🐻

Cassie sprinted off the bus and down her long driveway. Even in the daylight, she kept an eye on the orchard and dashed up the steps and into her house. She threw her backpack onto the couch and charged up the stairs to her room.

"Cassandra?" her mom yelled from downstairs.

"I'll be down in a minute, Ma!" she shouted, digging through her closet. Eventually, she found what she was looking for: a large yellow flashlight with a black handle. Her dad kept one in each bedroom in case the power went out. She checked the clock on the wall. Nearly four o'clock.

She charged back down the stairs and out the front door, the screen door slamming shut behind.

At top speed, Cassie made it to The Pit in record time. Darwin was already waiting. He had a messenger bag slung over his shoulder, with a two-liter bottle of Jolt Cola and a pair of plastic Coke cups with Max Headroom on them. Cassie thought Headroom was weird looking, but the commercials were funny.

"Hey," Cassie said, resting her hands on her knees to catch her breath.

"Hi! Why are you so sweaty?"

She noticed splotches of black grease all over his white t-shirt and jeans. The Los Angeles Kings Starter jacket around his waist was ripped on the sleeve, white fabric poking through the black material. The boy even had grease on his face. "I've been running since I got off the bus. What's your excuse?"

"I'm a working man," he said, smiling. "I changed the oil in an old Buick and then helped Mom install a new engine in a Geo." He flexed his muscles and muttered, *"Muy fuerte."*

Cassie nodded, impressed. "That's pretty cool, actually. Pour me some of that, wouldja?" She gestured to the Jolt.

"What's the flashlight for? Scared of the dark?"

She stuck her tongue out at him. *If you only knew.*

Darwin placed the messenger bag on the ground and pulled out the cups. He opened the bottle and started pouring. Cassie thought about the night before and wondered if telling him now or later would be the right move.

Screw it. "I saw something last night. In the orchard. After I left your house."

Darwin handed Cassie the cup. "C-c-c-c-catch the wave!" he said, mimicking Max Headroom.

Cassie stared at him and shook her head. "Anyway ..." She took a sip of Jolt. "There was something in the trees last night. It made like, a grumbling noise. Then when I saw its eyes, it screamed at me and I bolted home. I can't get those red eyes out of my head."

Darwin furrowed his brow and poured himself a cup of soda. "You're just trying to scare me. Nice try."

She shook her head. "You didn't hear anything last night? Maybe five minutes after I left?"

"Nope. I was helping mom set up a dresser upstairs."

"You would've heard this, man. It was *loud*. It was like a lion mixed with a Jawa from *Star Wars* or something. I don't know how else to describe it."

He finished his cup and poured another, then topped Cassie off. "Jawas have a high-pitched voice. Did whatever you think you saw have a high-pitched voice? Are you thinking of a Tusken Raider?"

She shook her head. "I don't know, dude. I don't know nerdy stuff like that. That was my brother's thing."

"Sorry. I'm just kiddin' around. Did you really see something in the orchard last night?"

Cassie nodded. "Something *big*."

"Like a bear?"

"No. Not like a bear. Bears don't get this tall. This thing, whatever it was, was humongous."

"How tall are these trees? Five feet?" Darwin was gesturing to the apple and peach trees of the orchard.

"Seven, most of 'em. It was taller than these by a couple feet."

"Nine feet tall?"

She shrugged. "I guess. It was dark."

They sat in silence a while, drinking soda and tossing rocks into The Pit.

"It stunk, too," Cassie said, breaking the silence.

"What?" Darwin asked.

"The thing in the orchard. It smelled really bad."

Darwin looked toward the forest beyond The Pit. Thick, green trees stretched around the eastern edge of the property. "Come on, let's go check out the woods by the house."

"You sure you wanna go?" Cassie asked.

He shrugged. "I dunno. What else are we gonna' do? You said you wanted to see if we could find any trace of the kids your dad chased away or whatever."

Darwin extended his hand and pulled Cassie to her feet. Together, they started toward the guest house, cutting through the orchard, walking for a while along the edge of The Pit. Darwin seemed lost in thought, as though he was mapping the orchard's terrain. Cassie liked watching the boy figure work out the geography of the orchard. He'd mutter to himself, gesturing from his position to the guest house first before turning his attention to the barn or the main house and nodding, as though creating a mental map in his mind.

At Darwin's house, he placed the messenger bag on the porch, along with the empty cups and bottle of Jolt. He then followed

Cassie to the border of the woods and disappeared into the gloom. The forest was thick near their home. So dark it always felt like night. She didn't venture in there often when she was younger, but the few times she did, she worried she'd never find her way out. Morgan was there to help her find her way home.

"What do these look like to you?" Cassie asked, pointing to a strange pyramid-like assembly of logs. Scattered along the ground were smaller logs, some broken in half with wide indentations like claw marks.

"Looks like a teepee or something," Darwin said. "Can you go in?"

Cassie tried to squeeze herself between the logs, but couldn't. "I don't think it's for shelter. Who would put this here?"

"Your dad said there were kids, right?"

Cassie knelt and tried to lift one of the heavier logs. She couldn't move it more than a few inches. "Maybe. Strong kids, I guess."

The two stood in silence, examining the structure and the larger logs and vines along the forest floor.

"Hey, I never thanked your mom for letting us move in," Darwin said as they stepped over vines and fallen logs in the forest.

"Oh, well ... it's no biggie."

"It was to us. Our old place got raided by police. They showed up and threatened our landlord. Said Lakeside didn't want a problem with illegals."

Cassie shook her head and stopped. She turned to Darwin. "I'm sorry that happened."

"Me too. But this house is so much better than our apartment. It's so big and ... well, it feels like a real home again." They walked deeper into the woods and the terrain angled upward, into the foothills and the mountain beyond.

"Is it like the house you lived in back in El Salvador?" Cassie asked between breaths. The hike was taking its toll, and she struggled to move through the dense underbrush.

Darwin shook his head. "No. Back home, we had to move a lot. The war going on and all. I was very little."

"What was that like?"

"The war or moving?"

Cassie shrugged. "Both."

"The war was scary. That's probably not a surprise. It was a revolution. My dad and mom fought on the front lines a lot. My mom was not at first, but she insisted. After Dad died, she stopped fighting, and we started working on getting to America."

Cassie held her hand up and they stopped. She brushed her dark hair from her face and looked into Darwin's eyes. She thought of Morgan in the desert. Shooting guns, hiding in bombed-out buildings. She didn't really know what he was going through, and the thought of her brother in danger sent pangs of anxiety from her toes to her stomach. She shook her head, clearing the cobwebs. "I'm really sorry, Darwin. I'm sorry that you lost your dad."

"Me too. He was funny. Like, he could make any situation funny. He and Mom would laugh all the time."

"That's awesome. He sounds like a cool guy."

"He was. I wish I could hear Mom laugh like that again."

Cassie felt drawn to the young man's pain and reached out slowly to take his hand. They held each other's gaze. She knew what was happening. She'd had crushes before. But this was different. Darwin was different. Sharing pieces of himself with her no boy from school ever had. Her fingers lingered close to his ...

Fa-koooom! An explosion from up in the mountains broke their shared reverie, and they looked upward. While they couldn't see much through the thick forest, they saw a puff of gray smoke disperse into the air.

"Guess we're not far," Cassie said, turning and starting up the hill again.

They hiked through the foothills into the deeper sections of the Dunderbergs. The mountains weren't as awe-inspiring as the Rockies or Appalachians, but they were beautiful, carving gray-purple into the reddening sky. Mount Cisco stood the highest, and Cassie promised herself she'd make it to the top one day.

Cassie reached a meadow and waited for Darwin to catch up. Wood-clearing machines, along with various tents and trailers marked *Williams Logging* crowded the area. There were a few people scattered around, most carrying wooden boxes marked with the *flammable* logo.

Cassie knelt and picked up a small rock at their feet. "See this?"

Darwin nodded.

"This is the kind of rock my dad found when you guys moved in," Cassie said, examining it. "The kind that was thrown at the house."

"You think maybe one of these workers did it?"

Cassie shrugged. She didn't see why it *couldn't* be one of the workers. It certainly made more sense than a giant monster in the woods near her house, after all. A monster she'd never seen before in all the time she'd lived there. "Maybe," she said, finally. "Maybe the explosion sent rocks all the way down to the orchard?"

"Is that possible? Seems awful far."

"I guess anything's possible," Cassie said with a shrug.

"What're they doing?"

"See that cave?" Cassie pointed to the gaping mouth of a cave behind one of the larger tents. "They're collapsing the entrances. They go down deep, into a mine system. So, they don't want anyone in there."

"That's what those explosions are," Darwin nodded.

"Yep. I only went into the mines once. With Morgan. Creeped me out. I hated it."

"I've never been in a mine. Sounds weird."

"It was wet. Smelled like moss. The further we went, the worse the smell got. I'll never forget it ..."

Suddenly, it hit her. She turned to Darwin. "The *smell*. Darwin, holy smokes."

"Hey, you two, get out of here!" one worker called as he began marching toward Cassie and Darwin.

The two sprinted off into the thick, verdant forest.

As the kids made their way through the thick woods, they listened to birdsongs and buzzing insects. The scent of flowers, greenery and moss hung in the air, and Cassie saw Darwin run his fingers along the fuzzy green side of a boulder once they came to a clearing.

"What were you talking about back there?" Darwin asked.

"When I was in the orchard the other night and saw that *thing*, I smelled something. It was the same smell as inside the cave when I was a little kid."

"You're still a little kid," Darwin said with a smile.

"Yeah, yeah, you know what I mean."

They continued walking, looking over the tall pines, firs, and other trees they could not have named. Cassie let her fingers graze along the large fronds of a vibrant yellow-green fern.

"You see anything weird?" Darwin asked.

"Nope. Not even any of those little rocks. Nothing at all. Just dirt, woods, bugs and birds." She paused and looked around, sniffing. She prayed she wouldn't smell whatever was in the orchard the night before. Thankfully, only hints of violet from the blue flag flowers that littered the area. "I gotta' pee," she said after surveying the area.

Darwin stared at her and Cassie gestured for him to turn around.

Unzipping her jeans, Cassie squatted behind a tree and relieved herself. "If I catch you looking, I'm going to deck you."

Darwin laughed. "I actually have to pee, too." She heard the rustling of leaves and imagined Darwin went somewhere nearby to take care of business. "Jolt always makes me have to go," he shouted once the rustling died down.

"Me too. My mom would have a cow if she knew I was drinking it," Cassie said. She pulled a small packet of tissues from her pocket, cleaned herself, and stood up. "She doesn't like me getting too much caffeine."

Cassie stepped out from behind the tree and looked around. The sun burned orange in the distance, intense light still beaming through the canopy of leaves above them. Darwin emerged from a large cluster of bushes, zipping his pants back up.

"What're those?" he asked, gesturing with a nod.

"What?" Cassie walked over to him.

"What you're standing in."

She looked down. Cassie traced enormous footprints along the soft dirt of the forest. They ran past where Darwin stood, into the thick brush.

"There's three sets of prints," Cassie said.

"Four," Darwin said, pointing. "Look at that one."

Cassie looked at where Darwin was pointing. A smaller set, not as noticeable as the others, but certainly larger than either her own or Darwin's feet, stretched around the tree Cassie ducked behind to pee in a semi-circle, then around another tree.

"Like it's playing," Darwin said.

"What do you mean?"

"It goes around the tree," Darwin said, making a circular motion with his hand. "Like whoever left it was doing Ring Around the Rosie."

Cassie noticed something small and rock-like mingled in the dirt. She knelt and picked it up, hard like a stone but darker and porous. *Not a rock*, she thought. "The fruit's not ripe yet. It's much smaller, but ... this is a peach pit. This isn't much bigger than a penny. Not ripe."

Darwin looked like he'd seen a ghost. He stood, frozen, staring at the tracks.

"*Sisimito*," he whispered.

"What? What'd you say?"

"Nothing. You think it's a baby?"

"A baby what?"

Darwin knelt and placed his outstretched hand within the biggest print. It was less than a quarter the size of the print. He looked up at Cassie, eyes focused. "We should get out of here."

Cassie sat on the porch steps outside her house. She clicked the flashlight on and off at Darwin, and he covered his eyes as he rocked on the wooden swing fastened to the overhang.

"What was that word you said before? 'Sissy'-something," Cassie asked, tucking her knees into her chest as the wind picked up, coaxing a shiver over her exposed skin.

Darwin stood and untied the jacket around his waist. He draped it over Cassie's shoulders and sat beside her. She inched closer to him, staring into the field of apple and peach trees.

"*Sisimito,*" he repeated. It hung in the air between them. "It's like ... a half-man, half-gorilla thing. Folklore from Guatemala. I have some family there."

"Half-man, half-gorilla. Like Bigfoot?"

Darwin nodded. "Yeah, that's what you'd probably call it. Yeti. Sasquatch. All those things."

She stared at him. "First *bruja* now, *sisimito*?" They both laughed and fell backward onto the porch.

"I wasn't scared, you know?"

"When?"

"When we were in the woods before. I wasn't scared. I was scared at school. In my bedroom last night. On the couch. After I saw those eyes. I was scared then. But not in the woods."

He looked at her. She nestled deeper into his jacket. It smelled like him. Hints of motor oil and some kind of cologne, musky and spicy. After a moment, she recognized it. *Old Spice*. The only other cologne she knew was Brut, her brother's go-to.

"If you weren't scared, then how *did* you feel?" he asked. Cassie was looking directly into his eyes. There was a hint of awkwardness between them. Cassie felt as if she were being watched. As if a thousand eyes were on *her*. Butterflies and anxiety coursed through her from her toes to her stomach.

"I felt at home," she said finally. "Like I belonged there. In the woods."

He smiled. "Maybe you do."

She nodded, fighting the urge to look away. The sun in the distant sky cast shadows in the orchard and glinted in his eyes. Cassie felt lost there. In Darwin's eyes.

"I better get inside. My folks are probably steamed at me," she said, sitting up. She shrugged off the Starter jacket and held it out.

He stood up and stretched. Cassie looked him over and thought in the fading light of the day he looked perfect. His tanned skin, long limbs and messy hair. He turned to her and waved, saying, "Keep it. It looks better on you."

She put the jacket back on as Darwin started east toward the guest house.

"You gonna tell your mom what we found in the woods?"

He stopped at the tree line and turned around. "I don't keep things from her, so yeah, probably."

"What do you think she'll say?"

He smiled. "That we're crazy."

CHAPTER FIVE

Cassie lay in Morgan's room playing REM's *Endgame* on his stereo. Krystal made dinner and they ate, even though Bernardo was absent. When Cassie asked where he was, Krystal shrugged and said she didn't know. It wasn't like her dad to miss dinner.

She tossed one of the rocks from the mountain up and caught it. Her dad had left it on the table beside his chair in the living room, so she snuck it into her pocket when she got home from hanging with Darwin. She thought about whatever it was in the mountain coming down, rocks in hand, for the sole purpose of throwing them at the guest house. *Why would they do that?*

Then it hit her. She sat up in Morgan's bed and looked out the window, past the forest that framed their property and toward the mountains. Mist slithered around the treetops. The occasional birdsong in the fading light. *That's it. That's your home. The caves.*

The cave system, which connected to the mine system, would make the perfect home for creatures looking to avoid detection. It made sense. If a habitat is disturbed, new territory will be sought. She'd read about it in textbooks. Habitat loss was common in areas of deforestation. Cassie thought of animals being pushed out due to the sealing of the mines. The noise, the influx of people, these things would certainly scare away native wildlife. Might even be enough to spook something as big as what she saw in the orchard that night.

Michael Stipe sang softly. Cassie bobbed her head along with the beat and thought about Darwin. She took a sniff of his Starter jacket and smiled. She worried enjoying the smell of the boy's jacket somehow made her a creep, but then figured if no one was around, it wasn't a big deal. She felt comfortable being a creep in the confines of her own room. Or rather, Morgan's, which had kind of become *her* room too.

"Hey kiddo," Krystal said from the door.

"Hey," Cassie said, sitting up. "What's up?"

Krystal shrugged. "Wanna' watch a movie?"

"Maybe."

"Where'd you get that jacket?"

"It's Darwin's. Don't be weird."

Krystal couldn't hold back any longer. "I'm not weird. You two becoming buddies?"

"I guess so. I dunno'."

Krystal crossed the bedroom and sat beside Cassie. "You miss Morgan a lot. I do, too."

Cassie leaned her head against her mom's shoulder. "Yeah. I wish he'd call again."

It had been almost a month since she last heard his voice. Her brother's unit had seen some combat. He was able to tell them that, but they hadn't sustained any losses. Some light injuries, but Morgan was fine. The more time passed between phone calls, the more Cassie worried.

"He'll call soon, sweetie," Krystal said, brushing a few stray strands of thick black hair from her daughter's face. "You're really turning into a beautiful young lady. You're not just my little cutie pie baby anymore."

Cassie stuck her tongue out, feigning disgust. "Mooooom," she groaned.

Krystal mimicked Cassie by sticking her tongue out and hugged her daughter hard. "I know, I know. It's so terrible to hear your mom tell you how beautiful you are and how much she loves you. Ugh, what a nightmare!"

They rolled back on the bed, laughing. *Shiny Happy People* trickled from the sound system. Krystal tickled Cassie without mercy. "Moooom, I'm thirteen, you can't attack-tickle me anymore!"

"Oooh, I love this one!" Krystal said, ignoring her daughter, rising and hopping around the room. Cassie loved watching her mom dance. She was a bit of a hippie in her youth and still bopped around like one with the right inspiration. On Saturday mornings, Krystal turned on the kitchen cassette player and jammed to bands like The Mamas and the Papas, The Byrds, and The Zombies. Cassie appreciated it but would never listen to *old people stuff* on her own.

Krystal took her daughter's hands and pulled her up from the bed. They danced for the entire song, laughing and just enjoying themselves. They spun in circles, bare feet kicking up Morgan's thin purple rug. It was torn in places and needed replacing, but that wasn't something Morgan would notice.

Cassie often danced with her mom as a little girl. They'd spend their summers with Morgan running around the orchard, having fun, picking apples and peaches, enjoying the literal fruits of their labors. Morgan carried a small radio, then a larger boombox as he got older, so there was always music to accompany their *frolics*, as Krystal was apt to call them.

As the song came to a close, they laughed and caught their breath.

"Look at my two favorite girls," Bernardo said from the doorway. "You two are too much!"

"Look what the cat dragged in," Krystal said, walking to him and planting a kiss. "Where've you been?"

He sat down at Morgan's desk. "Town. Talking to some hunters."

Cassie knew her dad had gone to Hollow Point Hunt & Tackle. It was the only place in town that catered to hunters. Since Resting Hollow, Lakeside, and the region of Apple Valley were more centered around seasonal tourism and *good hunting* had migrated further north, deeper into the Dunderberg Mountains and the surrounding forest, Hollow Point was the only game in town. Cassie had only been there once when she was little, and the owner, a grizzled outdoorsman and named Adriel, scared her so much she never went back. There were rumors he was of Algonquin ancestry, but that wasn't what she remembered about him.

He wasn't scary to look at, Cassie realized. It was the old man's eyes. They were light gray, almost white, and when she and Morgan had gone into the shop to buy bait for fishing, Adriel's eyes followed them around the store. He reminded Cassie of a vulture, ready to swoop down and carve up the soft flesh of something long dead. His wrinkled, scarred face and the various heads of defeated creatures mounted on the wall behind him underscored Cassie's anxiety. Then again, she was only seven years old with an imagination as vast as the orchards.

"About what?" Krystal asked.

Cassie sat on her brother's bed. She knew why her dad was talking to hunters. Had he seen something in the woods as well? He hadn't said anything, but Cassie needed to know.

"Dad, did you see something in the woods when the rocks hit the guest house? The day Darwin and Azura moved in?"

"What're you two talking about?" Krystal asked, looking from Cassie to Bernardo. "'Nardo, what rocks?"

He reached into his pocket and pulled the rock out. He tossed it to Krystal, who fumbled it. It landed on the rug with a light *thud*. She knelt and picked it up. Bernardo glanced nervously over to Cassie.

"We're going to put up some spotlights outside. Along the porch. The barn. The garage. On the guest house, too."

"Spotlights? Like motion sensor lights?"

Bernardo lowered his head and nodded slowly.

"Dad, what did you see in the woods that day?"

He looked up at Cassie and shook his head. "I don't know. Whatever it was kept to the shadows. The darkness. The forest is thick. I could only see its eyes through the leaves."

"Was it an elk? They can be dangerous, for sure," Krystal began.

"No elk. It was taller."

"A bear?" Krystal offered.

Bernardo shook his head. "Bigger. I don't know what I saw. Maybe I'm making it up, I don't know." Bernardo ran his tanned hands over his face. He looked exhausted. "That day, when the new tenants moved in, I saw something. I shouldn't tell you this, of course. I found a pile of meat. Like, imagine a deer or a bear or something ... just hollowed out." Bernardo looked around the room, as if searching for the words to describe the impossible image in his mind. "Like, when you scoop out the guts of a pumpkin. You put it on the newspaper and it sits there, right? Imagine that but with the insides of an animal. Just in a pile beside the husk of the animal itself."

He gestured to his stomach, his fingers looking more like claws. A hushed silence fell over the room and Cassie looked up, brushing the long, dark hair from her face.

"I saw what did it," Cassie said.

Her parents turned toward her and stared. "When, *Cucciola*?" Bernardo crossed the room and sat beside his daughter.

"Two nights ago. In the orchard."

"What did it look like? Why didn't you tell us sooner?" Krystal asked.

"I was hoping that maybe I dreamed it. I don't know. Darwin and I found tracks in the woods before."

"That boy knows about this?" Bernardo asked. Cassie couldn't tell if her dad was upset or worried, and his reaction confused her.

"Yeah. Don't be mad."

"I'm not mad, Cassandra. I'm just scared." Bernardo wrapped an arm around Cassie and hugged her. "All of our time here, I've never seen anything like that in those woods. I don't know what kind of animal would *do* that. Just ... pieces of things everywhere. Like a maniac was in there or something."

Krystal stood in the center of the room, arms crossed. "Should we call the police?"

Bernardo looked up at his wife. "That could be a problem with our new tenants, no?"

"God damn it," Krystal muttered. "You're right."

"Wait, how come?" Cassie asked.

"Well, Azura and Darwin aren't here *legally*, sweetie. So, if the police know they're here, they could be sent back to their country."

"Salvador Dali," Bernardo said, nudging his daughter at his terrible attempt at humor.

"*El Salvador*," Krystal corrected, rolling her eyes. "It could be trouble for them and maybe even trouble for us."

Cassie's cheeks burned. She didn't understand why the police would protect one group of people and not another, but she didn't know what to say. Instead, she put her head on her dad's shoulder and sighed. "What're we gonna do, Dad?"

"Lights outside on the houses and barn? Maybe we get a big, scary dog?"

"A gun would be better than a dog," Krystal said.

"Mom!"

"I know, I know. I guess we've always kinda' wanted a dog?"

"Have we?" Bernardo asked with a chuckle. "Back home, we'd have coursers to guard the farm. They'd keep the geese away. Though this ... *thing* might bigger than a goose."

"Coursers?" Cassie asked. "I don't know what that is."

"Like a mastiff, baby. A mastiff would be good. A bulldog. Pit bull? Something tough," Krystal said.

Cassie stared at her feet, then looked up at her mom. "Darwin and I think it's a monster. He said they have something like it back home in El Salvador. Or in Guatemala. *Sisimito*. It's like a big ape-man type thing."

Krystal laughed. "Like a yeti? Isn't that in the Himalayas or whatever?"

"Apparently, that's something different. Darwin knows a lot about this stuff. Weird stuff. Nerdy stuff."

Krystal smiled. "I bet he does."

Cassie rolled her eyes. "Maybe there're things like this all over the world and we just haven't really found them yet."

Bernardo rubbed Cassie's shoulder. "Tomorrow, I'll go pick up the sensor lights. Maybe you two go to the pound after school and find us a dog?"

Cassie looked up at Krystal. "I wish I was more excited about getting a puppy."

"Me too, sweetie," Krystal said, forcing a smile. "Me too."

CHAPTER SIX

The next day, Cassie and her mom walked up and down the kennel of the local animal shelter in Lakeside. They were looking for something large enough that it might somehow intimidate the enormous creature Cassie saw in the orchard what seemed like ages ago, but was only a few days.

The volunteer working at the shelter that day couldn't have been much younger than Morgan, and Cassie wondered if she knew her brother. The young woman leaned against the wall by the door of the kennel leading into the adoption area and examined her fingernails while Krystal looked into the cages.

"None of these dogs look tough," Cassie said. "I just feel sad." There were only four dogs in the entire kennel, and none of them were particularly large. The biggest, a Labrador with graying hair around its snout, rested his head on a tattered blanket and watched as Cassie and Krystal walked by. A metal sign on the door to its cage read *Jellybean*.

Krystal nodded. "Yeah, I really hate this. I hate this place. I just want to take all of them home."

Cassie looked up at her. "Maybe we can? Maybe if we take all of them, or like, a bunch of them and just let them roam around the orchard?"

Krystal laughed. "Well ..."

Cassie didn't think it was a bad idea. Expensive, maybe, but not bad. Her heart ached looking at the dogs in their cages. They were older, most likely abandoned by their former owners. Cassie held back tears at the thought of someone giving up their pet like that. It didn't seem right to her. Cassie was so young when her last pet, a cat named Truffle, died. She only remembered him through pictures. Krystal and Bernardo just hadn't replaced him and instead, they buried him in the backyard with a small slab of granite as a grave.

The other three dogs in the kennel included a pair of German shepherds who were apparently siblings, *Frick* and *Frack*, and a tiny chihuahua that looked more like a chew toy than an actual living creature named *Louise*.

"Look at this one," Krystal said, gesturing to the chihuahua. "I mean ... come *on*."

"She's cute. Maybe she's the ringleader of the whole organization?"

Krystal turned to the shelter volunteer. "We'll take all of them."

"I said to get *one* dog, not *four*, my darlings," Bernardo said from the cab of his pickup truck as three of the dogs ran around the orchard.

"We couldn't leave them there. You didn't see that place. It was awful," Krystal said, turning to Cassie. Jellybean sat at Cassie's feet, directly beside her. "Plus, they're all friends, we think. So, taking one away would be like punishing the other three."

"Why doesn't this one go play with the others?" Bernardo asked.

Cassie knelt and pet Jellybean behind the ears. He snuggled up and laid down in the dirt beside her, presenting his belly. With a chuckle, Cassie began rubbing the dog's ribs. "I guess he likes me."

"We can set them up in the old barn," Krystal said. "Not like we use it for anything, really."

Bernardo nodded. "Sure, yeah. Have they had their shots?"

"I think so. Guess we'll find out if Cassie gets fleas or heartworm or whatever," Krystal said.

Cassie looked up. "Heartworm?"

"Si, *Cucciola*. Tiny little creatures with teeth that eat their way through the valves and arteries of your heart," Bernardo said slowly, trying to sound scary.

"That's dumb," Cassie said, rolling her eyes. "Can Jellybean stay with me? Like, he can sleep in my room instead of the barn."

Krystal looked at Bernardo. He shrugged. "If it makes you happy, then sure. I just hope he's housebroken."

The family listened to the other three dogs bark and explore the new territory as the sun began to set over the mountains. A distant explosion froze the dogs in place, turning their attention to the mountains.

"I'll be glad when they're done with that nonsense," Krystal said.

Azura stood, drinking a Corona on the upstairs deck of the guest house as Bernardo stood on the opposite side on a ladder installing the motion sensor lights. Cassie and Darwin were below, each with a foot on the ladder to help keep it steady. Cassie wondered if it actually helped or if this was her dad's way of keeping his eye on her.

"I'm sorry that this is necessary," Bernardo said to Azura.

"No skin off my ass," Azura said, sipping the beer. Another explosion in the distance caught her attention. "I feel like they've been really hitting the mines and mountains hard the past few days."

"Must be close to finished," Bernardo said, screwing the wall mount into place. "This is waterproof, just so you know. No danger to you or Darwin, should it rain."

"That's good," she said, disinterested, eyes on the forest and the mountains. Cassie followed her gaze and saw a gray mist hanging low to the trees. "Looks like the fog's rollin' in. *Niebla*."

Bernardo turned. "The air is dry but it's cold. Been a weird season."

"Crops hurt by the cold?" Azura asked, placing the empty bottle on the wooden railing.

"They'll be okay," Bernardo said. "Maybe a little behind schedule, but they'll be fine soon enough." There was a hint of anxiety in his voice. Nervousness that made him sound younger somehow, smaller.

"What did your mom say about what we found the other night?" Cassie whispered, her eyes on Bernardo atop the ladder and trying to keep Azura from hearing her.

"Like I told you," Darwin began, matching Cassie's whisper. "She thinks we're crazy. But then she went and checked her rifle, so maybe we're not too crazy."

"Your mom has a gun?" Cassie asked. She'd never even *seen* a gun before walking past the ammo store, and the thought of one being on her family's orchard made her nervous.

"*Guns*, actually. She's got a rifle and a couple of pistols. Why?"

Cassie shook her head. "No reason."

Darwin smiled. "I like that you're wearing the jacket."

Cassie smiled at her feet, her cheeks warming. She'd been wearing Darwin's jacket almost exclusively since he gave it to her a couple of days ago. The second she walked in the door from school, she'd throw it on and spend the rest of the night making up excuses to her parents about why she was wearing it. She relied on the unseasonably chilly nights.

A bout of laughter above between Bernardo and Azura caught Cassie and Darwin's attention, and they looked up. Azura was drinking another Corona and Bernardo was, too. Cassie shook her head and scoffed, trying to hide her smirk.

"What's wrong?" Darwin asked.

"My dad's a lightweight. Anything other than vino, he gets drunk quick," Cassie said. "Dad, almost finished?"

Bernardo sipped the beer. "Of course, little one. Almost done."

He tightened another screw, then flipped a switch on the light. He leaned back a bit from the floodlight and waved his hand. The light came on, blinding him for a moment, and Cassie worried he might fall. He righted himself and shook the cobwebs loose, climbing down the ladder.

Once at the bottom, he looked up at the light.

"Bright, no?" he asked no one in particular.

The light clicked off. Cassie took a step and after a second, it clicked back on. "Works pretty good."

"Just gotta do the one on the barn, and we're finished," Bernardo said. "You two alright to help me?"

Darwin nodded. "Yes, sir."

Bernardo waved up to Azura. "If you have any trouble, let me know."

"Hey, Bernardo, why not let the kids go off and play? I can help you with the last one," Azura called from the porch.

"You sure?"

"Yeah, come on, me and Darwin have important business," Cassie said, pulling Darwin by the wrist and charging off into the orchard. She didn't wait for an objection, and instead vanished within the rows of apple and peach trees.

*   *   *

"I have a theory," Cassie said, tossing the rock up and down. She looked over the expanse of The Pit, surveying the broken machinery, glass, and more. "Ready?"

Darwin nodded. He dangled his legs over the edge of The Pit and looked up at her.

"I think the caves that we saw are their home. Like, the mines and stuff. Because the county is sealing them up, they have nowhere else to go," Cassie began talking fast. "And because it's been so warm, and the town's been cutting down trees on the mountain, they've got no choice but to come down from the mountain."

"How many sodas did you have today? You're talking really fast," Darwin smiled.

"I'm *serious.* What do you think?"

Darwin thought for a moment. "In my country, *sisimito* comes out of the forest when he falls in love with a woman from the towns. He takes her and she's never heard from again."

"That's so stupid," Cassie said, then joined Darwin along The Pit. "Maybe not stupid. I don't know. I don't know what to think."

"Maybe it's not *sisimito*, maybe it's just a big, weird man in the woods?"

"Somehow that's worse, right?"

Darwin laughed. "Before you got to the porch, your dad asked if I wanted a job this summer picking the fruit and maybe working the register at the stand."

"That's what I do, too. What'd you say?"

"Well, he actually told me that. I said that I would do it, too."

"Purely for the experience of working with fruit and learning how to use a cash register, right?" Cassie asked, stealing a look at him.

"Totally. That's totally why."

Cassie leaned her head on Darwin's shoulder, and they looked across The Pit towards the forest. An explosion from up in the mountain made Darwin jump and Cassie locked her hand in his. Slowly, mist began to form around the tops of the trees, the sky burning orange before finally going dark.

Chapter seven

When school finally ended, Cassie didn't feel the exhilaration that typically awaited her at summer break. Her usual summer of working the farm stand and helping pick fruit was on the horizon, but there was more to it than that. Morgan helped to occupy her in the summer. Helped create a spirit of adventure around every trip into the woods, into town, down to Bloch Lake. Fishing in the rivers of the woods was a favorite pastime of Morgan's and Cassie had grown to love it, too.

Without Morgan, there was no promise of summer, as she knew it, for Cassie.

The things in the woods only served to sever whatever hopes she had for a normal summer, too. Though they hadn't seen much evidence of them as school came to a close, in walking the perimeter of the orchard and venturing into the foothills and forest, Cassie and Darwin found nothing. The weather hadn't warmed much, and the county was starting to wrap up its closure of the mines in the Dunderberg Mountains. Things were almost back to normal. As normal as things could be without Morgan around, anyway.

Cassie and Darwin picked fruit, and even with his help, they were woefully behind the quota Bernardo expected. Usually, their fields were filled with additional hands, local kids from the college or high school, many of them Morgan's friends looking to earn a few extra bucks, but because of the lean season, all the work fell on Cassie, Darwin and Krystal. Three people to do the work of two dozen. Cassie would've thought it was unfair if she didn't know that her mom and dad needed her.

Louise, the chihuahua, along with Frick and Frack, ran through the orchard while the three of them worked in different sections, Krystal taking the section closest to The Pit, with Darwin taking the apple trees closest to the guest house. Cassie worked the section nearest the barn, and the dogs did their best to distract her. Not Jellybean, though. He sat stoically beside her, sniffing the ground, his ears twitching at things Cassie couldn't hear.

Since Bernardo installed the lights, there hadn't been much action. A bear came through one Tuesday night but didn't so much as bother the trees, opting instead to knock over their garbage can and steal some chicken bones before running off into the woods. Cassie watched the bear closely from her window. It had become part of her routine, staring out the window each night, hoping she'd catch a glimpse of whatever it was in the orchard again. But nothing ever came.

Each time she and Darwin were in the orchard, Cassie kept one eye on the forest while they picked apples and peaches. At first, Darwin kept his eyes on the forest, too, but as the weeks rolled on, his focus shifted to the work in the orchard and with his mother, fixing cars.

Azura didn't forget. Though she didn't completely *believe* Darwin's stories about the thing in the woods, she kept the rifle under her bed and the pistol tucked into the back of her jeans while she worked. She knew better than to ignore warnings about a predator in the area. Imagined or otherwise.

Krystal worked herself to the bone in the orchard. Trying to make up for the lack of staff took its toll on her. She was up early and in the orchard before anyone else, Louise the chihuahua at her side, nipping at her heels most days.

Bernardo would have late night conversations with Adriel, not returning until after dark. Long days in the orchard, followed by long nights at Boney Brom's Tavern in town, talking to groups of hunters, Cassie worried about her dad as he drove home. It wasn't a long drive, but still, she worried. Bernardo never drove drunk, but all it took was one extra glass of wine on the wrong night. Sometimes, Cassie would sit on the steps and listen in on her dad's phone conversations. Though busy, the orchard had been quiet, but she knew her dad was troubled. Bernardo hadn't seen what Cassie saw, but was still shaken by the mound of guts and raw meat in the woods. Bernardo took to calling it an *offering* after one late night conversation with Adriel.

Cassie lifted the phone in her parents' bedroom and actually heard Adriel's side of the conversation one night. His voice was gruff and he spoke in short, measured words. It matched him physically and every time he said something, Cassie felt a shiver up her spine, remembering how he scared her as a little girl.

"They do that," Adriel said. "They left that for you. An offering. Maybe a challenge."

"A challenge for what?" Bernardo asked.

There was silence on the line and Cassie held her hand over the receiver in the hopes her dad and Adriel couldn't hear her. She held her breath and waited for the hunter's response.

"Your land, Bernardo."

🦍 🦍 🦍

Cassie wondered if she was delusional. Maybe she hadn't really seen anything at all, and maybe she was just over-tired that night in the orchard. *But the footprint. The peach pits.*

"Could be anything, Jellybean." The Labrador looked up at her a moment, then continued its vigilance, ears twitching and adjusting in the daylight.

"What do you hear, boy?" Cassie waited for an answer that would never come. "Silly."

Jellybean's head shifted as though focused on something far off. The dog turned toward the nearby forest. After a moment, the dog rose on its haunches and straightened its back. The dog began to grumble. Low, more of a rattle. Cassie turned to him.

"Jellybean?"

Frick and Frack sprinted up beside Jellybean. They were joined by Louise a moment later. All four dogs stared in the direction of the Labrador and watched in silence before adding to the chorus of growls.

"Easy, easy ..." Cassie started, placing her nearly full basket of fruit down. Cassie turned toward the snarls and growls and watched as the forest shifted in the breeze a moment before a cluster of birds erupted from the treetops. They fanned into the sky, chirping and singing loudly.

Jellybean began barking and Cassie jumped at the vicious sound. The two German shepherds joined in, then Louise, with her tiny but ferocious yip. Cassie was surprised by the amount of noise the four dogs made for what seemed like nothing.

"Hey, come on," Cassie said softly, scooping Louise up. "Come back to the barn."

Jellybean's barking became more frenzied and eventually, Frick and Frack's did too.

🦍 🦍 🦍

That night, Cassie lay in bed. Her open window faced the mountains closer than her brother's and she kept peeking toward it, a cool breeze ruffling the drapes. Jellybean lay beside her, eyes closed, breathing deeply. The Labrador eventually calmed down that afternoon, and the twin dogs went back to the barn with no issue. Louise didn't have much choice, and once she was placed down in her doggy bed, she dozed off almost immediately.

Cassie caressed Jellybean's head absently, her eyes on the window.

Ughhhhraaaaaaaaaaaa.

Cassie bolted up in bed at the noise. It was further away than the night in the orchard and went on a full two seconds longer. She ran to the window looking over the fields of fruit trees visible from her bedroom. At first, she didn't see anything, until finally, close to The Pit, she noticed movement. Large figures, dark in the moonlight, lurked on the opposite side of the large trench of broken metal, glass, and debris.

The dogs in the barn barked but she couldn't see from her room. She did her best. She leaned out the window and craned her neck, catching a glimpse of its far side. No commotion disturbed the shadows there, but the dogs were restless.

Cassie turned her attention back to The Pit and lumbering figures. Their heights varied, with the tallest towering two feet above its companion. The third, smallest figure was much shorter, but in the shifting moonlight filtered through tree branches, an accurate description was impossible to glean.

Her dad charged down the steps of the house and a second later, the motion sensor light along their back porch bathed the area in bright yellow light. Cassie ducked under the windowsill, worried he might see her, and when she raised her head above the ledge of the window, he was sprinting through the orchard on his way to The Pit.

"Daddy," she whispered, anxiety overtaking her. She threw on a pair of jeans, her sneakers, and Darwin's jacket and ran down the stairs, Jellybean beside her.

"Where are you going?" Krystal called from the bedroom.

"Daddy's outside! Those things are by The Pit!"

"What?" Krystal shouted. She, too, got dressed and followed Cassie down the stairs.

Cassie and her mom ran as fast as they could through the orchard, following Bernardo. The darkness loomed heavy around them, even with the motion sensor lights illuminating a good portion of the closest perimeter of the fruit trees. Jellybean tore off ahead, bridging the distance to Bernardo.

"Jellybean, wait!" Cassie shouted, struggling to catch her breath.

Krystal and Cassie followed Jellybean's shrill, panicked bark. They heard the other dogs in the barn, too. No, not *in* the barn. The barking was louder, no longer muffled by the wooden walls of the barn itself. The barking had become frenzied snarls and viciousness that Cassie had never heard from an animal before.

"You hear that?" Cassie asked. She turned abruptly in the row and started toward the barn. "I'm gonna' go check on the dogs!"

"Cassandra!" Krystal screamed. But Cassie was gone before her mom spoke her name.

Breaking through the rows of trees, Cassie froze in her tracks. Fractured wood littered the ground, and a sizable section of the barn's wall was missing. She thought it looked like something from an old Warner Bros. cartoon, like when Wile E. Coyote or Yosemite Sam smashed through a wall leaving a body-shaped hole behind. Where those outlines were clean and distinct, this was more violent. The wall was broken from the ground to about two feet above Cassie's head. What would that have been, seven feet? Taller? The scent of mildew hung in the air, and Cassie recoiled at the smell.

She moved slowly to the opening in the wall and peered inside. In the far corner of the room, Frick and Frack huddled, shivering in the darkness. The barn was empty with the exception of the dogs' beds, toys, food, and water bowls. The ladder that led to the hayloft sat in the center of the room, and Cassie's attention was drawn to the lightless gloom there.

"Frick, Frack, come here ..." she whispered, extending a hand to the two dogs. They whimpered and ducked their heads, hiding from her.

A *crunch* from outside the barn, along the back, where the motion sensor light was. Cassie slipped from the darkness inside the barn and moved along the outer wall in slow motion.

Once at the edge of the wall, Cassie took a deep breath and peeped around the corner. Perfectly illuminated by the spotlight was a creature sitting in what Cassie's kindergarten teacher called *crisscross applesauce*. The hairy thing dined noisily on a slick-looking piece of ... something.

As Cassie's eyes adjusted, she noticed more detail. Five fingers. A nearly hairless face, with dark flesh visible. A wide nose. Large eyes, colorless in the shadow cast by its colossal frame. Five toes on a pair of massive feet.

The creature she saw in the orchard was bulky. Wide, even. This thing, however; was lean. Not as skinny as Darwin, but Cassie thought that if a kid *like* Darwin put on a gorilla costume with a little bit of padding, it might look like this.

The creature flicked something away and it landed at Cassie's feet. She knelt to get a better look. A bloody collar. *Louise.* She gripped it tightly and fought the sob building in her chest.

Cassie began to hyperventilate. The creature raised its head and made *whoop* noises over and over in sharp succession. Cassie raised a hand to her mouth, covering it so she couldn't possibly make another sound, and listened for movement behind the barn. She did her best to stay hidden around the corner, peering out the slightest bit to see the strange animal behind the large converted barn.

She watched videos of gorillas in science class and documentaries on the Discovery Channel. *This* felt far more human than ape. Cassie grimaced at the *crunch* of the creature dining on what was left of Louise. Reaching into the pocket of Darwin's jacket, she fingered the rock from up on the mountain. At first, she did so out of nervousness, but then a plan began to take shape.

She needed to get this thing away from the barn and the other two dogs. Needed to scare it off somehow. She wished she had her brother's hockey stick or, better yet, one of Azura's guns. Cassie looked off in the distance and saw the guest house, its motion sensor light on as well. She could make out Azura on the back deck, scanning the orchard.

Ughhhhraaaaaaaa from off in the distance made Cassie jump. A shuffling noise from behind the barn trapped her breath in her lungs. Certain the monster would come around the corner and rip her to shreds, Cassie clenched her teeth and waited for the worst.

It didn't come. She exhaled and looked behind the barn again. Nothing, as if she had imagined it. She kneeled over the bloody stain in the dirt that was once Louise. There were a few hairs smeared withing the gore, and a dozen footprints led into the nearby forest. The motion sensor light clicked off and Cassie waved her hands, terrified to be in the dark. When it came back on, she thought she could see the creature lurking in the woods barely fifteen feet away. Its eyes reflected the spotlight.

"Get out of here!" Cassie screamed, rising suddenly and waving her arms as if scaring away a raccoon. "Go on! Leave us alone!"

A rumble from the forest, like an approaching storm, suggested it was preparing to roar. It did the same thing in the orchard, only this one's pitch was higher. Maybe it was younger. The height didn't match. A kid? Cassie couldn't stop staring at the two eyes peering back at her, glittering in the glow of the spotlight. She focused on them, detail taking shape. They were set far apart, to match the enormous head of the creature, and shifted slightly, as though what loomed in the forest was ready to pounce at a moment's notice.

Propelled by anger over Louise, Cassie reared back and hurled the rock, hoping to nail the creature right between the eyes. Morgan always teased her about her aim, how she was a sharpshooter with things like straws, crumpled up pieces of looseleaf paper and other things that never did much damage.

When the creature in the woods whimpered and blinked furiously, Cassie knew her aim was true. "Get away!" she screamed into the darkness. "I'll kill you if you come near here again!"

With another *aghroooowooo*, the eyes blinked again rapidly in the darkness. Cassie didn't know where this newfound bravery came from. Maybe losing a dog she was beginning to love to a *thing* that broke through the wall of the locked barn as if it was made of straw. Whatever it was, it had sent the girl over the edge. Deep down, she hoped she hurt the creature in the darkness.

Only one eye glowed in the gloom of the woods, and it slowly receded, disappearing. Cassie waited until the thing was finally gone. She hyperventilated, adrenaline causing her body to go cold. Her hands trembled, the bloody collar jingling lightly in her hands.

When she felt safe enough, she dropped to her knees and wept, her face slick with tears.

After some careful coercion, Cassie led Frick and Frack out of the barn and through the orchard, holding their collars tightly. She couldn't risk the two shepherds running off. And as crazy as it sounded, she didn't want the twin dogs to know that Louise was dead. Cassie didn't know if dogs felt the pain of loss, as humans do. She just hoped to spare the two dogs the knowledge of their friend being dead for as long as she could.

At The Pit, in the general direction Jellybean and Krystal headed in pursuit of Cassie's dad, she looked for any sign of her parents or the Labrador.

"*Cucciola*!" Bernardo shouted, running to her. He wrangled the two shepherds, holding their collars. "Where have you *been*?"

"One of them was by the barn," Cassie said between sobs.

"Another one?" Krystal said. "There were three over here. We only saw them a moment. They took off into the woods once Jellybean showed up beside your dad."

Jellybean trotted to Cassie and licked her hand. "Good boy, Jellybean."

"What did the one by the barn look like?" Bernardo asked, kneeling and wiping tears from his daughter's face.

"About your height. Skinny. It wasn't the one I saw in the orchard that night."

"The ones that were over here were ... big," Krystal said, her eyes on the forest. "Really big."

"Maybe nine feet," Bernardo said. He took a deep breath and turned to Cassie, as if something had finally dawned on him. "*Cucciola*, are you okay?"

To her mother, Cassie said, "It killed Louise. It was *eating* her."

Krystal recoiled and bit her lip to stifle her tears, but eventually, they won out. She cried softly to herself, still holding the two German shepherds by their collars.

Jellybean nuzzled against Krystal's leg. She chuckled and sat down in the dirt. The Labrador rested his head in her lap and she shook her head, a look of exhaustion on her face.

"I hit it with a rock. Right in the eye, I think," Cassie said.

Bernardo smiled, his eyes welling up. "That's good, baby."

"The dogs stay in the house," Krystal said. "I don't want them roaming the orchard unless we're out here with them."

"What good would that do?" Bernardo asked, shaking his head. "You saw how big they were. You think *we're* a threat to them?"

"I don't know, 'Nardo. I just don't know," Krystal said.

Nothing was said for seconds that felt like minutes. Cassie looked from her mom to her dad, waiting for a plan, an answer. Something. The silence hung in the air, suffocating. Cassie thought it strange that she couldn't hear any noise from the woods, nothing that would indicate a wildlife in the area at all. No owls hooting. No crickets. Nothing.

"There's a big hole in the barn. That's how it got in," Cassie said, finally. The silence was too much for her. "Broke through the wall."

"*Porca puttana!*" Bernardo muttered. "Sorry, little one. I'm not mad at you."

"I know, Dad. What are we going to do now?"

Bernardo thought a moment. "I think maybe we need some help."

After returning to the house with Frick, Frack, Jellybean, and Krystal, Bernardo and Cassie took a walk over to the guest house. They found Azura on the front porch, cigarette in her mouth, rifle resting in her lap. Beside her was an empty Corona bottle and another that was half full.

"That loaded?" Bernardo asked.

"Always," she said, taking a drag from her cigarette. "I saw them tonight. Figure that's why you're here."

Bernardo nodded. "They killed one of my dogs."

Azura shook her head. "You okay, Cassandra?"

"Yes, ma'am."

"She threw a rock at it," Bernardo said, patting Cassie on the back. "Maybe hit in the eye. I don't know. It all happened so fast."

The woman smiled, wrinkles sprouting at her eyes again. Her skin was like a roadmap, and Cassie wondered just how old Azura was. "Good girl. Eye for an eye."

"Your son okay?" Bernardo asked.

"He's asleep, I think. Missed all the *action*."

"That's good. I just wanted to check on you guys. I have an idea of what to do, but this is your home, too. I don't want to do anything without you being okay with it."

Azura stood and leaned the rifle on the column beside her. She finished her Corona and stepped off the porch. Cigarette in mouth, she looked at the forest and nodded to herself. "You ever hunt anything before?"

"Duck. Quail. Back home in Italy, that's about it."

She glanced toward Cassie, then back to Bernardo. "Ever kill a man?"

"No," he said quickly. "Why do you ask me that?"

Azura snuffed the cigarette out on her boot, then dropped it into the empty Corona bottle. "These things, *sisimito* as my boy thinks it is, or *sasquatch* or whatever you want to call it. It's more *man* than it is *animal*. You see their eyes? Different than an animal's eyes, right?"

Bernardo furrowed his brow and shook his head. "I don't–I mean ..."

"They do. Their eyes are almost human. But bigger. Their eyes glow like a cat's, though," Cassie said.

"Very good. The girl is smart. I see why my boy likes her so much," Azura said with a smile that wrinkled her face. "*Primer amor.*"

Cassie shrunk away, cheeks warming.

"Azura, what are you trying to say?"

"It can be hard to pull the trigger on a man. But you have to remember, these things aren't *all* man. They may play tricks on you. The way they look at you. The noises they make. Back home, they take people. You never see them again."

"That's what Darwin told me," Cassie said.

"He's right. I can teach you to shoot, Bernardo. You come here. You and the girl. Krystal, too. We need to teach you to defend yourselves."

Bernardo looked down at Cassie. "I don't know if I want Cassandra learning–"

"If not now, when?" Azura asked, cutting him off. "These things are *here*. They've come onto *your* property. The fruit missing from the trees, you think that's deer? When was the last time you even *saw* a deer, Bernardo?"

"I–I don't know ..."

"Exactly. How about tomorrow morning, we go into town? Me and your family. Maybe go to the hunting store run by that old man. We go pick out some things to help keep your family safe. You come here after lunch. I could show you and you some stuff."

Azura jaunted up the front steps. She was the coolest person Cassie had ever seen, other than Morgan. She thought Azura and Morgan would make a good team.

"Does Darwin know how to shoot?" Bernardo asked.

Azura smiled. "He's his mama's son."

🦍 🦍 🦍

The following morning, Cassie lay in her brother's bed staring at the ceiling and listening to The Church's *Gold Afternoon Fix* on cassette. A family trip to Hollow Point Hunt & Tackle was on the horizon, and Cassie wasn't excited to see Adriel again. It had been years. She recalled the last time. Adriel's sharp gray eyes following her around the store like a bird of prey.

Krystal was downstairs, preparing a simple breakfast, and Cassie heard her dad shuffling around the bedroom. He moved quickly, almost frantically, throughout the room, and Cassie wondered what was going through his mind. She did that a lot lately. Wondering. Thinking. Worrying.

While her mind was predominantly focused on the creatures in the woods, the lingering thought of not having contact with her brother for months gnawed at the back of her mind. Calls had been regular before he deployed. She knew it would be sporadic, but not like this. Cassie watched the news every night and saw footage of the war in Iraq. She knew it was silly to imagine seeing her brother fighting in the footage, but the anonymous men she saw on the television were all *somebody*'s brother. Son. Father.

The thing behind the barn. Was *that* somebody's son, brother, or father? It was decidedly more human than animal, yet at the same time, Cassie was confused by the creature. *If it were a person*, she thought, *then wouldn't it be able to talk?*

She shook the thought from her head, realizing there were plenty of humans who didn't speak. She learned about *Genie,* a feral child who didn't speak due to neglect and abuse. This was in Biology last year during a lesson on evolution. Cassie found the topic interesting, and in fact found all of Biology interesting. Earth Science was another story. Rocks and dirt and layers of the planet weren't as thrilling as the study of life, and her grades reflected her disinterest.

Maybe they're just feral people? She shuddered at the thought. *People aren't nine feet tall.*

"*Cucciola,*" Bernardo said from the door. "Almost time to go, yeah?"

"You think the dogs'll be okay while we're gone?"

"We'll put them in the basement. They'll be okay, I promise."

Krystal opened the basement door with a creak. The darkness below always gave Cassie a lurch in her chest and her mind always went to Tim Curry lurking in the shadows, dressed as a clown. Morgan loved to taunt her with jeers of *You'll float, too.* It never failed to crack him up. As much as watching late night horror movies with her brother freaked her out, she missed it.

Staring into the abyss of their basement brought all the feelings of a late-night horror movie fest back. The darkness didn't bother the twin German shepherds as they both followed Krystal down the stairs. She placed the bowls of food and water down and turned back towards the top of the steps.

"Come on, Jellybean," Krystal called from the basement.

Cassie looked down and saw the Labrador sitting beside her. He stared at Krystal, then looked up at Cassie. "What's wrong, boy?"

"Cassie, lead him down here, would you?"

Cassie took Jellybean by the collar and took a step down into the basement. "Come on, Jellybean."

He wouldn't budge. Cassie pulled harder, trying not to hurt the dog, but he wouldn't move from the spot. He eyed Cassie and whimpered, nudging her with his head. Krystal took a few tentative steps up from the basement. "What's going on?"

"He's not moving, Mom."

Krystal ascended the steps. Once at the top, she took Jellybean by the collar and attempted to lead him down the steps. "Come on, boy." No dice. Jellybean pulled from Krystal's grasp and moved himself closer to Cassie, tensing up and sticking close to the young girl's side.

"I don't think he wants to leave your side, *Cucciola*," Bernardo said from the porch. "Let him come along. Azura's waiting outside."

In the back of the truck, Azura and Cassie sat together, Jellybean curled in Cassie's lap. Azura's cigarette dangled from her mouth and Cassie wondered how it stayed in place.

"My boy's taken a liking to you, kiddo," Azura said as they rolled down the highway toward Resting Hollow.

Cassie lowered her head, letting her hair cover her face, suddenly feeling a rush of heat to her cheeks. Azura reached over and brushed the hair aside.

"You shouldn't hide your face, Cassandra. You're a pretty girl. Look just like your mama," Azura said, taking a drag off her cigarette. "The world sees this. You need to see it, too."

"Thank you," Cassie said. She smiled nervously and continued petting Jellybean. "You really think I look like my mom? People always tell me I look like my dad."

"Maybe a little, sure. But you have your mom's *vibe*, you know?" Azura blew a smoke ring. Cassie watched it hang in the air a second before dissipating. "When you have a certain vibe, it affects you."

"You have a vibe, too."

"Oh yeah? What's *my* vibe?"

"You're so cool," Cassie said quietly.

Azura laughed. "If you say so, kid."

Azura high-fived Cassie and lit another cigarette. She offered one to Cassie. The girl thought about it a moment and reached for the pack, but drew her hand back, shaking her head.

"In life, little one," Azura began, taking a puff. "You have to take what you want. Take the shot you want. Make the move. I was younger than you when I had my first cigarette."

Cassie looked down, her hair falling in her face. Remembering Azura's words, she raised her gaze and brushed the hair away.

"That's right," Azura said with a smile. "Don't hide from the world, otherwise the world will hide from you. *Dime con quién andas, y te diré quién eres.*"

"What does that mean?" Cassie asked.

"It's like saying that you're known by the company you keep," Azura said. "How do you say? People see you for who you are, and for who you spend time with. *¿Consíguelo?*" She caught herself and smiled. "Sorry. Understand?"

Cassie nodded. She felt close to Azura. There was something so magnetic about the woman, that Cassie felt if people judged her by who she spent time with, then spending time with Azura must by default make her the coolest person in town.

The car ride to Hollow Point Hunt & Tackle didn't take long. Once they entered town, Jellybean sat up and looked around, eyeing the people in the area. Cassie caressed his back, rubbing behind the dog's ears and down his tense haunches.

"It's okay, boy. We'll be right back," Cassie whispered.

Cassie climbed out of the back of the pickup and Jellybean followed. He walked over to Cassie and resumed his place beside her.

"No, silly. You have to stay here in the truck."

"Maybe we tie him to the bench over there?" Bernardo asked, pointing to a wooden bench set up outside the store.

Cassie noticed the town was bustling. Folks shopped, ate breakfast at the various restaurants and just enjoyed the beautiful summer day, despite the chill in the air. Cassie led Jellybean to the bench by his leash and started tying it around the leg. In a flash, Jellybean pulled away, the leash going with him and falling limply to the sidewalk.

"Hey," Cassie said. She took the leash in her hands again and attempted tying it, but Jellybean wouldn't stay put. He pulled at the leash, taking a section in his mouth for added leverage.

Bernardo walked over. "He's not gonna' be tied up. He wants to stay beside you."

Cassie looked up at her dad. "Why?"

Azura snuffed out her cigarette. "He loves you. Maybe he's protecting you. I don't think the old man inside will mind a dog walking around the store. Come on."

Krystal opened the door and the tiny bell chimed above. Bernardo walked in and kissed his wife on the cheek. Cassie and Jellybean followed, and she looked around the store. Azura followed next.

Fishing poles, nets and more hung on the walls, and there were racks of fishing vests, hats, and other hunting apparel. An enormous glass case sat in a U-shape in the center of the store, filled with smaller weapons like knives, pistols, and more with their price tags scrawled in dark, barely decipherable handwriting.

"Adriel?" Bernardo called. "You here?" The store was dark, with the exception of the illuminated glass case at the center that served as the focal point of the room. The rows of camouflaged hunting clothes all seemed to bleed into one another, and the orange safety vests were about the only flash of color in the entire store.

Azura stood at the gun case, looking over the stock of weapons.

Cassie stood near a row of military surplus equipment, including Meals Ready to Eat, boots and other stuff. "Think this is what Morgan eats every night?"

Krystal walked over and checked out the MRE's, examining their contents. "Chicken alfredo in sauce? Meatball surprise? God, I hope not."

Cassie held one up. "What about *beef product in gravy*? Doesn't that sound delicious?"

The two shared a laugh as Adriel emerged from the back office of the store. "Sometimes those meals might surprise you. When I was in Korea, those little packets gave us a little taste of home that we needed."

The old man emerged from the doorway; his gray eyes bright in the dim light of the store. His hair was short, cropped military style, the way Morgan's was before he shipped out. Only Adriel's was white. His thick eyebrows stood out like pale caterpillars against his dark skin. He came out from behind the register and approached the family.

Cassie was especially interested in the Algonquin pictures and information Adriel displayed on the walls. She'd always enjoyed going to the Historical Society and learning about the people who originally settled the region. Their history, their beliefs, all of it was so interesting to Cassie and Morgan.

"Bernardo, good to see you again," he said, shaking his hand. "What brings the whole family down here?"

Krystal smiled and shook Adriel's hand next. "I'm Krystal, this is Cassie. And I hope it's alright that Jellybean's in the store."

"Of course," Adriel said, kneeling and petting the dog. Cassie was surprised the old man was able to move as confidently as he did. Older folks in the Hollow, especially those who had worked manual labor their entire lives, often shuffled around, their bodies beaten. She imagined her dad would be the same way one day. Maybe even her mom. Adriel looked at Cassie. *Those eyes.* "Jellybean's a good name. You name him that?"

Cassie shook her head. "No. That's the name that was on his cage at the shelter."

"Shelter dog. Good. You don't want a purebred designer dog. Jellybean looks healthy. Strong," Adriel continued petting the dog. "I think I have some venison jerky in the back for him. Let me get it real quick. You guys take a look around and I'll be right back."

With that, Adriel rose and ducked back into the office out of sight.

"What do you think of this one?" Bernardo asked to no one in particular, looking in the glass case at a shiny pistol, the words *Colt All-American* emblazoned on the side.

Azura came around from the other side of the counter and looked at it. "That gun is trash. Not reliable. *All-American.* Bah!"

Adriel emerged from the back and gave Jellybean a few strips of jerky. "There ya' go, boy. Enjoy that."

"What's 'venison'?" Cassie asked Krystal.

Sharing a concerned look with Bernardo, Krystal shrugged and stammered to find an answer. "Well, it's–umm ..."

"Deer. Bagged them myself," Adriel said.

Cassie swallowed hard. "Deer meat?"

Adriel nodded. "There's too many in this region, Cassie. It's good sport. Good hunting," the old man began. "I keep some of the meat for myself, share the rest with others who need it more than me."

"Venison is delicious," Azura said, not looking up from the gun case. "I'd like to get some of that jerky before we go."

"O'course! Oh, I know you!" Adriel exclaimed, waving his finger. "You're that mechanic everyone talks about. The one who can fix anything."

Azura smiled. "I don't know about that. Maybe not *anything*."

The old man waved his hands. "Nonsense. I been meaning to contact you. I got an old Chevy that needs some love. A real *tank*, you know? Been broke down a while now."

"That's what you get for buying an American car, man," Azura said. They shared a smile and Azura winked at Cassie. "I'm happy to take a look, bring it up to the orchard Monday, yeah?"

Adriel nodded. "I can do that. So, Bernardo. You thinking about pulling the trigger on something today? Pun absolutely intended, of course."

Bernardo shook his head. "Maybe, Adriel. That's why I brought Azura here. She knows this stuff better than me. I figured you two could figure out what would work best for all of us."

Adriel looked Krystal and Cassie over. "Wait, you mean, *all* of you?"

"We've got a pest problem at the orchard," Azura said. "It's big."

"I've heard. Been a long time since anyone's seen one in these parts. Last time was ... hell, I think Carter was in office."

"How do you know about this?" Krystal asked.

"Well, your husband called and we talked about it," Adriel said, glancing at Bernardo. "The Algonquin would see them in the old days. But again, not for a long time. They stick to the mountains. The deep woods."

"Not anymore," Bernardo said.

"That offering," Adriel said. "Maybe it really *was* a warning."

"In my country they just come into town. No warnings. No nothing. They take people. Never see them again," Azura said. "*Cabrones.*"

Adriel nodded. "When some of the Algonquin migrated west, their caravans would get ambushed. Most of the time late at night. Sometimes, though, in the daytime." Adriel ran a hand through his short, white hair. "They say it was a time of great cold then. Even though it was spring and summer. Records show that it was the coldest the region ever was."

"You think they're entering our land because it's cold on the mountain?" Krystal asked, furrowing her brow.

"Cold means food is scarce. If the trees aren't budding, mushrooms not growing, flowers not blooming, it all has an impact."

"They're chopping down a lot of trees up there. Near the mines and caves," Cassie said.

"Darwin told me you guys didn't see any wildlife when you were up on the mountain. No food would mean they're hungry. The orchard's like a free buffet for them," Azura said.

"Killing them isn't advised," Adriel said. "They're physical beings, but spiritual as well. They have ties to the land. Anything that upsets the natural order isn't good."

Azura rolled her eyes. "They're *animals*. Predators. They deserve a round between the eyes. Natural order or not, I'm going to kill one of those things if it comes back."

Bernardo shook his head. "What do we do?"

Azura nodded toward a row of rifles on the wall behind the register. "Those might do the trick."

The wall was packed with rifles of all sizes. Other than the colors, Cassie couldn't tell the difference, even as Adriel and Azura ran through the different models and companies from Ruger to Marlin to Smith & Wesson. A few hours later, Cassie's eyes began to glaze over at the different specs and figures associated with each rifle, its pros and cons, and more.

Krystal held a silver Ruger pistol. "This is the one for me, I think."

Bernardo held a lever-action black rifle in his hand. "Guess we're a Ruger family now?" He chuckled and held the rifle slightly away from his body, as if it was a snake that might bite.

Cassie looked around the case. "Do I get one?"

"Absolutely not," Bernardo said, placing the rifle on the counter beside the register.

"'Nardo, you brought her here for a reason, no?" Azura asked. "We've spent a long time talking about it. She needs to know how to protect herself."

"I don't want her playing with these things."

"Dad, it's not *playing*. It's *learning*. Azura's right. If those things come onto our property again, we *all* need to be ready. Not just you three."

"Four," Adriel said. Everyone turned and looked at the old man. "Maybe I come out there? Set up a tent near the border of the woods and the orchard? Keep an eye on things for a few nights?"

"I can't ask you to do that," Bernardo began.

"You didn't," Adriel said, placing a hand on Bernardo's shoulder. "I offered."

Bernardo shook his head slowly. "Adriel, I don't know if I can ..." he began. He leaned closer to the old man and lowered his voice. "I don't know if I can afford all of this."

Adriel smiled. "Listen to me. We can make it work, okay? A payment plan. A few bushels of those amazing apples of yours."

"And if you bring that old Chevy up, I can get her singing for you," Azura said. "Maybe that'll help the cost?"

"Thank you, Adriel. We can put some money down today, if that's alright?" Krystal asked.

The old man nodded. His gray eyes beamed.

Cassie said little on the ride back to the house. Azura, too. Before they left town, they stopped at Caldor to get some blank cassette tapes. Cassie wanted to be ready the next time those things came around. They weren't quiet. She needed a record of their noise. If for nothing else, at least to play for Morgan when he got home from Iraq.

Cassie held the three pack of tapes in her hand and thought about the guns. She'd never really heard a gun fired before outside of the movies. She worried she'd be scared. Worried that if those things came around, they'd do more than kill one of the dogs. Worried they'd hurt her mom or her dad. Worried that they'd hurt Jellybean. Or Darwin.

Looking at Azura, she imagined that the woman would never let one of those things even *close* to Darwin to hurt him. She'd die before that happened. Cassie wondered if either of her parents could protect *her* the way Azura could protect Darwin.

CHAPTER EIGHT

Cassie, Bernardo, Krystal, Azura, and Darwin spent the afternoon setting up empty Corona bottles on a section of fence that bordered the backyard of the guest house, a remnant of a fence that once ran the entire length of the property. The folks who owned the orchard before Bernardo took it over tore it down, but left some segments standing.

Azura balanced a cigarette on her lip, rifle slung over her shoulder. Krystal stood beside her, feet planted, arms extended with her hands tight on the pistol.

"Safety off," Azura said.

Krystal flipped the safety off and aimed at the empty beer bottle.

"Whenever you're ready, breathe through the shot." Azura held her breath as Krystal squeezed off a round, blasting the bottle to pieces. It was the fourth bottle Krystal had nailed on the first try, and Cassie worried her dad was feeling shown up by his wife. Every time she broke a bottle, Bernardo shook his head due to either embarrassment or amazement.

Darwin, drinking a Mountain Dew, sat next to Cassie on the porch. He offered her the bottle and she took a sip.

"Thanks. How come you didn't tell me you could shoot a gun?"

"Didn't really come up," Darwin said with a shrug.

"I guess. Would be good to know, though." She offered him the bottle back. Jellybean rested between them while Frick and Frack lapped at a bowl of water next to the front door of the guest house.

He took the bottle and said, "Sorry. What was the hunting store like?"

Cassie watched Azura set up two more empty bottles on the fence. Krystal flipped the safety back on and pretended to blow the smoke out of the barrel like in the old westerns they sometimes watched. Bernardo smiled and shook his head, unslinging the rifle from his shoulder.

"I guess it was kinda' neat. I used to be scared of the owner. He's got these eyes, you know?"

Darwin shook his head. "We all have eyes, *chica*."

"No, like ... not nice eyes like you," she said, cheeks flushing. "I mean, like, umm ... you know, I just ..."

"I get what you're saying," Darwin smiled. "I think you have nice eyes, too."

Cassie heard Azura's voice in her head. *You're a pretty girl. The world sees this.* Cassie lifted her head and brushed the hair from her face. "Thanks," she said, blood in her burning cheeks inching toward her earlobes. They sat in silence a moment, watching as Bernardo fired a round that was very wide of the bottles. He cursed in Italian and threw his hands up in frustration.

"Your mom's a good shot at least," Darwin said finally. They shared a laugh.

That night, Cassie and Darwin watched a movie from the living room floor. On screen, a group of men, one of whom dressed as a cowboy, battled bizarre looking aliens. Cassie reached into a bucket of popcorn and took a handful as Darwin finished his fourth Mountain Dew of the night.

"I don't understand this movie," Cassie admitted. "But it's really cool."

"Those are the Hong Kong Cavaliers. They're like a rock band, scientists, *and* superheroes. They're my favorite. I've been watching this all week on HBO."

"You get HBO?" Cassie asked, a little jealous.

"My mom rigged the cable box so we get *all* the channels," Darwin said with a proud smile.

"Man, she's so cool," Cassie said. She looked toward the kitchen and saw her parents at the kitchen table with Azura, talking. She couldn't make out words, but their gestures were sharp and serious. Azura made them dinner after practicing shooting, a quick meal of beans, rice, and salad, then dismissed the kids with a bucket of popcorn.

Jellybean lay asleep under the coffee table, snoring louder than the movie at times.

Darwin looked at Cassie. "I didn't say this before but ... I'm sorry about your little dog."

"Me too. My mom loved her. She carried her around a lot after we got her."

"That sucks. You said you hit the one that did it with a rock, right?"

"Yep," Cassie nodded. "Right in the eye, I think. I hope it's blind."

"Me too," Darwin said softly.

In the distance, they heard a sound. Siren-like and from up on the mountain. Cassie and Darwin bolted to the windows that faced the mountain range, scattering popcorn over the floor.

"Get upstairs!" Azura shouted from the doorway.

"But Mama, we can help!" Darwin whined.

"No, *niño*, *sube ahora*!" Azura's voice was stern and authoritative. She meant business.

With that, Darwin took Cassie's hand and led her up the stairs. When they were halfway up, Cassie turned and watched her mom, dad, and Azura slip out the front door, guns ready.

"Mom? Dad?" Cassie called as she and Darwin reached the top of the steps and started toward the back bedroom.

Once in the room, Darwin flipped the light on and stepped over to one of the pairs of windows along the far wall. Cassie followed and took position at the other unoccupied window.

The motion sensor light clicked on as Azura emerged from the right side of the house, rifle across her body. She moved slowly, taking careful steps, eyes locked ahead of her. Bernardo and Krystal appeared from the left side of the house walking together, Bernardo's rifle aimed toward the forest while Krystal kept the pistol pointed toward the ground.

Azura saw the light of the bedroom windows cast on the yard and turned to face the kids. She raised her hand and dropped it sharply. Darwin ran to the switch and flipped the lights off.

"What're you doing?" Cassie asked, her voice frantic and just above a whisper.

"Lights out. Mama wants the lights out."

They watched in silence as their parents crept closer to the tree line. Cassie noticed again the forest had gone silent. She could hear Darwin whispering to himself, repeating something in Spanish, low and rhythmic. Even in the dark, from the glow of the moon outside, she could see he was fingering his dad's necklace.

Cassie placed a hand on his shoulder. "It's okay," she whispered. Darwin nodded and slowly, he lowered his hand from the necklace. Cassie reached over and held it in the dark.

Down on the lawn, Azura directed Krystal and Bernardo with hand gestures. Shockingly, Bernardo understood and, after kissing Krystal lightly on the cheek, he took a few cautious steps away. They were creating a line, all of them armed and advancing slowly toward the woods.

Rughhhhraaaaaaaa, the sound came from far off. Darwin squeezed Cassie's hand tighter.

"Santa mierda," Darwin whispered in the dark.

"It's okay," Cassie said. "We can still see them. Don't get scared. I'm not scared. They're going to be alright." She reached into her pocket, withdrew the ChatBoy and removed the tape she picked up at Caldor. She cursed herself for not putting it in the ChatBoy sooner, but she carefully took her brother's tape out and slipped the blank cassette in. Cassie extended the microphone of the recorder and pressed the red *RECORD* button before placing it on the windowsill.

The two watched, holding their breath as their parents advanced still closer to the forest. Internally, Cassie worried her parents were too far apart. The skinny one she saw the other night could slip between the two of them, or God forbid, advance on them quickly and attack before they could even react. But Cassie knew she had to keep it together. For Darwin. For her parents. Even for Morgan. He would be out there with them were he here.

Don't worry about Morgan. Morgan's in the desert eating meals in packets. Mom and Dad are dealing with monsters.

For a long time, the only sound Cassie could make out was her heart pounding. She was sweating, racked with anxiety. Not just for her parents and the creatures lurking just beyond their land's border, but because this was the first time she ever held hands with a boy. Morgan didn't count. So much happening all at once and Cassie felt guilty for enjoying holding Darwin's hand while their parents were slowly walking toward the unknown.

Suddenly, a scratching at the door made both kids jump. It was loud and frantic, almost desperate. "The dogs!" Cassie shouted, running to the door and opening it quickly. The dogs dashed into the darkened room. She returned to her spot at the window and extended her hand, but Darwin's hands were on the windowsill as he watched with bated breath.

"They're going to be alright," Cassie whispered again.

Azura stopped near the thicket of bushes that gradually grew into thick trees that lined the property. Krystal did the same, then Bernardo. Cassie's parents glanced from each other to Azura, waiting for her to make a move.

"Don't go into the woods," Darwin whispered. "Not now. Not in the dark."

Ughhhhraaaaaaaaaaaaaaaaa! Another roar from the woods. This time, much closer. Louder. Clear.

Bernardo craned his neck, trying to get a better look at something in the forest. "I think I see something!" he shouted to Krystal and Azura. He stepped over a hip-high bush.

"No! Stay put!" Azura shouted.

"But I think I see it!" Bernardo yelled back.

"What's going on?" Darwin said, his voice quaking. "Mama! What's happening?"

Azura turned toward the window and raised a finger to her lips, silencing him. Without warning, one of the creatures broke through the thicket of bushes, shouldering Azura out of the way like an NFL linebacker. She crumpled to the ground, her rifle flying ten feet away toward the house. The creature moved fast for its size and the children jumped as they watched it explode from the thick greenery.

"Mama!" Darwin screamed.

Bernardo and Krystal ran toward Azura. The creature stood, thin and hairy, with large breasts, gray fur with a slightly hunched back. The back porch motion sensor light illuminated it, providing more detail than Cassie could make out the night before.

"*Sisimito* ..." Darwin whispered, eyes wide and terrified.

The gray creature lumbered over Azura's body, raising its hands high and bringing them down hard. With lightning reflexes, Azura rolled away before the enormous mitts of the creature could crush her.

"Shoot!" Azura screamed, scrambling for her rifle.

Krystal raised her pistol and squeezed off five quick rounds. The sound of the gun firing sent Cassie ducking below the window. Darwin remained standing, watching.

"Get down, Darwin!" Cassie shouted. The dogs in the room started barking at the sound of the gunfire. They ran around, trying to get out the windows and failing.

"Mama!" Darwin screamed.

Cassie peeked over the lip of the windowsill as Azura regained her footing, rifle in hand. She aimed carefully and fired at the gray-haired creature. Cassie gritted her teeth at the *CRACK* of the shots and reached over, putting her hand on Darwin's. He was crying and twirling the charm on his necklace. Cassie jolted at each shot, which sounded like the end of the world.

Bernardo closed the gap with Krystal and raised his rifle. He fired, and Cassie noticed the creature didn't react, so she figured his shot was wide.

Ughhhhraaaaaaaaarrrrrrrrrr! From the woods, long and sustained, the sound claimed everyone's attention. The gray-haired creature stumbled back toward the trees holding its chest. Cassie noticed the creature's haunches rising and falling sharply, clouds of breath escaping from its mouth and nostrils at a rapid pace in the cool night.

A chorus of *whoooop-whoooop* from the deeper part of the orchard caught Cassie's attention, as well as Bernardo's. Krystal raised her pistol and fired again, four more rounds. The gray-haired creature stumbled forward a few more feet, then keeled over face-down at the edge of the tree line.

Bernardo ran to Krystal and said something Cassie couldn't hear, then darted toward the orchard.

"Dad!" Cassie screamed, running to the door and flinging it open. Jellybean followed, and they sprinted down the stairs. Cassie nearly tripped as she bounded off the bottom step onto the landing and flung the front door open. What stood on the porch before her was something from a nightmare.

That smell ...

Easily nine feet tall. A wall of dark black-brown hair was the thing from the orchard. Yellow-red eyes glared through the gloom. In its arms was a tree's worth of apples and peaches. The dark leathery flesh of its face was pulled tight across its skull, and Cassie swallowed hard, wrestling with the reality of this impossible beast.

It roared, propelling Cassie back into the house, tripping on the bottom step leading upstairs. With a bark that sounded more like a scream, Jellybean leapt at the creature, sinking teeth into its arm. The fruit dropped and scattered across the back porch. Jellybean dropped, ducking a wide swipe of the creature's claws.

"Jellybean!" Cassie screamed.

From around the corner of the house, Bernardo appeared. He raised his rifle and fired, the bullet lodging into the column of the porch. Jellybean frothed at the mouth, placing himself between the monster and Cassie, directly under the doorway. The creature ducked its head, placing one enormous claw on the doorframe and tearing it out easily.

Another gunshot. This one landed. The creature's face contorted in agony and it backed out of the doorframe, Jellybean still barking and frothing at the mouth. Jellybean nipped at the nearest ankle, then ducked away as an enormous claw failed to find its mark a second time.

Cassie lurched toward the door as the creature dashed from the porch, hand on its lower back, making a light *whoop* noise as it moved. She noticed two other shapes in the distance and pointed toward them.

"Dad! Over there!" Cassie screamed.

Bernardo raised his rifle and fired in the general direction of the shapes moving through the orchard, breaking the property line and disappearing into the woods. He raised the rifle again and fired at the large creature from the porch, but it had already disappeared back into the gloom of the forest.

Cassie took a tentative step onto the porch and gawked at the claw mark on the doorframe. Four sharp indentations with a massive chunk of the frame missing. She found the missing piece a moment later, laying on the porch. She picked it up, marveling at how heavy it was and passed it to her dad.

"You okay, *Cucciola?*"

Cassie nodded. Jellybean nuzzled her legs. There was a little bit of blood on its muzzle, which streaked her calf. Darwin appeared in the doorway, flanked by Frick and Frack.

"I think they killed the one in the back."

Cassie, Darwin, and Bernardo joined Krystal. She stood twenty feet from the dead creature, shaking. The gun lay at her feet, and she couldn't control the shivering that was rattling her body. Bernardo placed his rifle down and embraced his wife. The second his arms wrapped around her, Krystal began crying.

Azura knelt over the creature. Its gray fur blew softly in the breeze and the motion sensor light's beam could barely reach it. There was just enough light to see that it was definitely female and definitely dead. Its side and back were riddled with bullets, small holes from Krystal's pistol. *Mom really is a good shot*, Cassie thought, stepping closer.

"Cassie, no," Krystal whimpered, holding Bernardo tightly.

"Your mama's right," Azura said, raising her hand to keep Cassie away. "You shouldn't see this."

"One of them was on the front porch. The red-eyed one from the orchard," Cassie said.

Azura rolled the creature over onto its back. She spotted the rifle wound on the creature's chest and noticed it had blown a portion of its chest clean off, leaving a five-inch hole where the rest of the chest should be. Thick red blood oozed from the wound and Cassie could see muscle deep in the opening, torn and jagged. She felt a pang of sickness rise in her throat but kept it down. She turned away from the gory, still bleeding wounds and approached her parents.

"Are you okay, mom?" she asked, wrapping her arms around her mom and dad.

"It's adrenaline," Azura said. "Perfectly natural. Just ride it out." Azura's fingers ran along the wound on the creature's chest. "I think this one is older. The gray hair. The looser skin. See how the flesh sags? Like a human woman." She held her fingers, now slick with dark blood, up to the light of the motion sensor light.

"That's enough," Bernardo said.

Azura stood and wiped her hand. "We got one. These things aren't special. They're not superhuman."

Azura pulled the pistol from the back of her jeans and squeezed a round off between the already-dead creature's eyes. Cassie and her family jolted at the sound.

"See? They're just animals. Like us. *Flesh and blood*," she said, stepping closer to the family. "Animals can be killed."

Azura placed her hand on Krystal's shoulder.

"You did good tonight. You all did," she said, looking first at Krystal, then at Bernardo.

"The big one broke the front door, Mama."

Azura faced Darwin. "Is that right?" She turned back to the dead creature near the tree line. She stared into the woods a moment, raised the pistol into the air and fired off another shot. "*Hijos de puta!*"

With that, Azura turned and spit on the still, dead body.

🦍 🦍 🦍

After a discussion on what to do with their quarry, it was determined that it might be best to drag it into the barn. Darwin had taken to calling her "Old Gray". Azura tied a chain around Old Gray's legs, backed her Chevy S-10 up, and fastened it to a winch in the bed. Bernardo helped crank the winch, hoisting the seven-foot-tall creature into the air.

Cassie thought it looked like a slab of meat from the butcher, hanging and waiting to be cut into steaks. She and Krystal hurried through the orchard to the barn as Azura, Darwin, and Bernardo slowly drove along the dirt drive.

With the barn doors open, Azura backed the Chevy inside, Old Gray's body lifeless, arms outstretched and resting on the flat cab of the truck. Blood dripped from its wounds, pooling in the corner of the bed, and Cassie recoiled when she caught a glimpse of the reddish-black flesh of the creature's open chest wound.

"The smell ..." Krystal said, putting her arm around Cassie.

"I know, right? Why do they smell like that?"

"I don't know, sweetie."

Bernardo climbed out of the truck, followed by Darwin. Azura stepped out from behind the wheel and looked over their quarry.

"We should take pictures of her," Darwin said quietly.

"What?" Bernardo asked. "Why?"

"No one knows these things really exist. If we take pictures, then people will know once and for all that they're real."

"He's right. We've got that old Polaroid camera in the basement. Darwin, why don't you and Cassie go get it then come back here?" Krystal said.

Azura pulled a Corona out of the small cooler in the truck bed and twisted the top off. She handed it to Bernardo, then opened another for herself.

"This wasn't a twist off," Bernardo said to himself, staring at the bottle.

Azura tapped the neck of his beer and took a swig. She opened another one and handed it to Krystal. "You're a helluva shot, Krystal."

Krystal smiled. "Kids, go get the camera. Be quick about it."

At the house, Cassie and Darwin made their way to the basement. When Cassie opened the door, she didn't think about the tricks her brother used to play on her. It was as if the silly games of their youth no longer mattered. Knowing there were actual monsters in the world made Cassie forget about fictional clowns lurking in basements, whether they were played by Tim Curry or not.

She flipped the light switch and Darwin followed her down the steps. Jellybean, too.

They searched through the large unfinished basement, moving cardboard boxes of old clothes, broken equipment, and seasonal decorations out of the way. With a sudden flash, Darwin let Cassie know he found the camera.

She smiled. "Stop that. We don't know how much film is left," she said. "Save some for Old Gray." Cassie made sure to put every ounce of sarcasm into the creature's name.

"What? You don't like the name?" he asked, taking the photo from the camera and shaking it in the air as it developed.

"It's not bad. What about the one at the front door? What do you call that one?"

"I didn't get a good look. I was thinking maybe 'Big Red' because you said it has red eyes."

A shiver went up her spine. "Yeah, that's pretty good."

Darwin looked at the photo in his hands. It was nearly finished developing. In it, Cassie peered into a cardboard box, her long, dark hair framing her face. She looked determined and curious.

"You're really pretty," Darwin said.

"It's not a bad picture."

"Not just in the picture," he said softly. "I really like holding your hand."

"I do, too."

He shifted from one foot to the other, his hands wrapped around the camera. "Would you maybe want to hold hands while we went back to the barn?"

Cassie smiled, a little embarrassed. She nodded.

🦍🦍🦍

The walk back to the barn was almost the most unreal moment of the night for Cassie. They walked through the rows of peach and apple trees hand in hand in the moonlight. It was like a million ridiculous movies Krystal had made Cassie watch. *Not as corny*, Cassie thought. Anxiety blossomed in her stomach as they walked, and she wondered if Darwin felt it, too.

"Hey," Cassie said, before they broke through the fruit trees near the open barn doors.

Darwin stopped. "Yeah?"

Azura's words echoed in her mind. *You have to take what you want. Take the shot you want. Make the move.*

"I really like you, okay?" she said after what seemed like an hour of silence between them but was probably only two seconds.

"I really like you, too."

In the moonlight, Cassie could tell Darwin was smiling. She hoped he could tell she was, too.

🦍 🦍 🦍

In the barn, Cassie spotted Azura smoking a cigarette. That wasn't much of a shock, but what really gave Cassie pause was that Krystal was, too. She'd never seen her mother smoke before, yet here she was, puffing away like an old pro.

"Listen, I had a life before you and your brother were born," Krystal said with a chuckle.

Darwin raised the camera and snapped a photo of Krystal with the cigarette in her mouth. Bernardo laughed and took the camera from the boy. He aimed it at Old Gray and started snapping from different angles.

"Azura, Krystal, stand next to it," Bernardo directed.

They obeyed, standing to either side of the body. Cassie thought her mom looked so cool flanking Old Gray with Azura on the other side. Azura held her rifle up, the butt resting on her hip, her head tilted slightly upward, looking down the bridge of her nose at the camera.

"That's how she's posed in her photos from back home," Darwin whispered to Cassie. He reached over and squeezed her hand. "She looks happy."

"They both do. They look badass," Cassie said. She was hit with a pang of sadness for the creature in that moment. This thing. *Old Gray.* Yes, it attacked them. Yes, it was scary. But there was something human about it. Or at the very least, something very much like a primate. A cousin to humanity, then. This *thing* was a mix between ape and human and watching Azura and the others treat it like it was just some animal they killed felt ... wrong.

"Cassandra, Darwin, come here!" Azura shouted. They sat beside Old Gray in the truck bed.

"Looking good, kiddos!" Bernardo shouted, snapping away.

After a few more photos, Bernardo thought it important to take close-ups of the creature's face, hands, and feet. He then finished the roll of film with Azura opening the creature's mouth to take pictures of its teeth. They were human-like with sharper, pointed molars. Cassie thought the teeth looked like the gorilla skulls she saw at the Bronx Zoo when she visited two years back.

"Damn," Azura said, running a finger along Old Gray's right fang. "Sharp as hell."

Bernardo nodded. "I think this gizmo's out of film."

Azura continued examining Old Gray's teeth. She ran her fingers along the creature's skin, picking with her nail at points. Azura took a small Swiss Army Knife from her back pocket and stabbed into Old Gray's back. The knife stuck in place until Azura pulled it out. She leaned close to the wound and brushed the creature's long, gray hair aside for a closer look.

"We can't be the only ones to ever kill one. It wasn't easy, but ... all the guns in this country? All the guns in the world? The hunters? The rednecks out in the woods? No one's *ever* killed one before? How's that possible?" Azura said.

"What do you mean?" Bernardo grabbed a duffel bag from a nearby shelf and placed the camera and photos inside.

"Their flesh is thick. Krystal's rounds did damage for sure, but it maybe would've survived if it got away. Look here."

Azura pointed at the knife wound. Cassie, Darwin, and Krystal walked over and were eventually joined by Bernardo. Even Jellybean got in on the action. Azura then spun the creature around on the chain and pointed at the bullet wounds. Smaller holes dotted the creature's back and side, trails of red-black blood oozing from them. Cassie noted that inside the hole, she could see the blood-stained round standing out goldish in color from the dark flesh and meat around it.

Azura turned Old Gray around and pointed again at the knife wound.

"My knife is small, but for any of us, this wound would require stitches. For this old girl, though ..." Azura trailed off.

"Their skin isn't like ours," Darwin said. "At least not entirely."

"*Órale*," Azura said, tousling Darwin's hair. "Even my rifle. It put her down, sure, but if a person got hit with this round, it would tear a much bigger hole in 'em."

"We've got two rifles. Two pistols. What else do we need?" Bernardo said.

Azura gestured to Krystal. "I think we need her to learn how to use your rifle."

Krystal smiled. "I'm down."

"Wait a minute, I hit the big one!" Bernardo objected half-heartedly.

Azura put her hand on his shoulder. "'Nardo, that's like hitting the broad side of a barn with a tennis ball. I counted what? Three? Four times you fired that thing?"

"Four or five, I guess ..." Bernardo sighed.

"You hit him *once*. We need better than twenty percent."

"If it was four times, it would be twenty-five percent, sir," Darwin said. He looked around the room. Krystal tried to stifle her laugh and failed.

Bernardo smiled. He handed the rifle to his wife. "I'm not a proud man," he said.

"You just need more practice," Krystal said, taking the rifle from him and slinging it over her shoulder.

That night, after examining the damage to the guest house's front door, it was decided that Darwin and Azura stay in the main house until it was repaired. Azura refused, but admitted she'd feel better if Darwin stayed with them. Before they left the guest house, Azura leaned in close to her son's ear and whispered something Cassie couldn't make out, but was sure had to do with her.

Back at the main house, Frick and Frack roamed the upstairs hallway while Krystal and Bernardo helped Darwin settle into Morgan's room. Cassie watched from the doorway and felt annoyed at first, but realized that it made sense. It *was* an extra bedroom after all.

"Good night, Darwin," Bernardo said, patting the boy on the shoulder. "Come on, *Cucciola*, let your boyfriend sleep."

"He's not my ..." Cassie began, a wave of heat rushing from her neck to her temples. She glanced at Darwin. "Good night."

"Good night, Cassandra."

Bernardo ducked into the master bedroom after planting a kiss on the top of Cassie's head. Krystal shared a knowing look with Bernardo and walked Cassie to her room. As she tucked her in and drew the curtains, Cassie could tell she wanted to tell her something.

"What's wrong?" Cassie asked.

"I know you and Darwin are getting close. But I don't want to hear you sneaking into Morgan's room tonight. We're all amped up from everything that happened, but I need you to act like a lady."

"Gross, Mom. 'Act like a lady'?" Cassie squinched her face, disgusted by the phrase. "I'm tired, mom. I just wanna go to bed."

Krystal changed the subject. "Do you have any questions about what happened tonight? You know it's okay to be scared, right?"

"No questions. And I *was* scared. When you started shooting. That's when I got scared. But then it went away."

"I was scared, too. Thought I peed myself, actually."

"Maybe that's what that smell was?"

Krystal recoiled, making a face of mock offense, and kissed Cassie on the cheek. "You little brat. Get some sleep. I know it won't be easy, but we have to try, okay?"

"Good night. I love you, Mom."

"You better," Krystal said with a wink before rising from the bed and walking toward the bedroom door. "Good night."

Krystal flipped the light switch and ducked from the room, closing the door behind her. Cassie took the ChatBoy off the table and pressed Play, lowering the volume as much as possible so her parents in the next room wouldn't hear. Before sleep finally took her, she listened intently to the low sound of gun-shots, the roar of the creatures, the shouting of Azura, Darwin, and everyone else.

Cassie lay in the darkness, staring at the ceiling. Side A of the cassette ended and she clicked the ChatBoy off. Crickets screeched, and owls hooted like ghosts outside. Nocturnal creatures that were normal this time of year. Nothing that sounded like a siren. The usual nighttime sounds.

Nothing that sounded like a nightmare.

CHAPTER NINE

Adriel arrived the following morning, his pickup truck loaded with camping and hunting gear. Bernardo was like a kid on Christmas as he led the old man to the barn. Krystal stood beside Azura, both smoking cigarettes in the morning sunlight.

Cassie sat beside Darwin on the hood of Morgan's El Camino.

"What do you think he's gonna' say?" Darwin asked.

Cassie shrugged as Adriel waved to Azura and Krystal, who opened the doors of the barn to welcome him inside. After a moment, Cassie heard him curse loudly before stepping quickly out of the barn, leaning forward on his knees and inhaling deep gulps of fresh air.

"Come on," Cassie said, hopping off the hood of the car and starting toward the barn. Darwin followed her.

Bernardo eventually joined Adriel in the sun beside the old man's truck. He placed a hand on his back and offered him a bottle of water.

"Do you know what you've done?" Adriel asked.

"Yeah, we killed one," Bernardo said. "They won't come around here anymore now. Not after we *killed* one and shot another."

"You shot *another* one?" Adriel looked from Bernardo to the kids, then to Azura and Krystal, who stood beside the open barn doors.

"I hit one with a rock right in the eye," Cassie said, a hint of pride in her voice.

Adriel took a deep breath and gestured toward the mountains and forest. He muttered something Cassie thought was a curse and sighed, turning back toward Bernardo. "That creature in there. I know you think it's just an animal, but it's *part* of the environment. I tried to tell you this. It's more than just a 'monster in the woods'."

"Not anymore, it's not," Azura said. "Where *I* am from, these things take women and children in the night. Take them deep into the woods and we never see or hear from them again."

Adriel shook his head. "These things were here before us. They'll be here *after* us. That *means* something."

Azura snuffed out her cigarette and lit another. "It means they're like cockroaches. They can be killed."

"You're playing a dangerous game here. They will come for that one."

Krystal furrowed her brow. "What do you mean?"

"You think it's some magic or something?" Adriel began. "Why we never find their dead? They *eat* their dead."

Azura made a disgusted face. "How very *spiritual* of them."

Bernardo interjected, "Adriel, what would you have us do? They keep breaching our borders. Taking our fruit. They killed our dog. Nearly killed Azura last night."

"Bernardo, there are consequences. Just like how we pushed further into their domain, pushed them further into the forest, the mountains. Now, maybe we pushed too far."

"And they're starting to push back," Krystal said.

"Cassie has a theory about them living *in* the mountains. In the mines. In the caves," Darwin said.

Adriel nodded. "The Algonquin believed spirits inhabit the mountains and forest. That they are only ever seen when they *want* to be."

"But we know they're flesh and blood. If they were a spirit, wouldn't they just disappear last night?" Bernardo said.

"I suppose so," Adriel said. "Maybe they were always just good at keeping themselves hidden from our eyes."

Azura stepped forward and took her sunglasses off. "When my people were fleeing the cities and going into the jungle to fight, we'd use the caves to get around. Sometimes we'd set up in them. Not long-term, but maybe these things did go long-term in there once the white man started developing the land."

Cassie nodded. "What better way to stay out of sight than to hide in dark caves?"

Adriel turned to Bernardo. "She's a smart one, your little girl."

"Takes after her mama. Adriel, we didn't mean to upset the nature of this place. This is our *home*. They killed our dog. They can't just keep coming here and eating my livelihood."

"I understand," Adriel said, thoughtfully. "Everything in balance. Everything has a reaction. I worry about what they may be planning next."

"Whatever they have planned, we have to be ready. They caught us off guard last night," Azura said, eyes unfocused as she lost herself in memory.

"How so?" Adriel said.

"This one was keeping us busy," Azura said, gesturing to the barn. "The other ones came into the orchard to get food and disappear before we really knew what was happening."

"That right? This one was a diversion? That's what you're saying?"

Azura nodded.

"The one in there is older but not as big. Well, not as big as the two other ones," Krystal said.

"I think they're a family," Darwin said. "Old Gray is the grandma. Big Red is the daddy. The other two, maybe Big Red's mate and their child."

"How do you know all that?" Adriel asked.

"Cassie's description. She's seen three of them."

"I haven't seen the one he thinks is a mate, but there's at least four of them."

"We saw that one. Not as big as the biggest one, but maybe seven, maybe eight feet tall," Bernardo said.

Adriel shook his head. "Your family has seen something that almost no one on this planet has. Now there's four of them. The nature of the mountain. The forest. It's all ... it all *has* to be out of whack."

"How could we know? How could *anyone* know?" Krystal asked.

"The logging, the closing of the mines. It all makes sense. Holy smokes," Adriel said.

The old man sat down on the bed of his truck and sighed. He looked at Cassie.

"I never thought I'd see the day," he said, shaking his head. He turned to Bernardo. "I'll set up between your house and the guest house. My tent. My camp. I need to use your phone. I may have something that could help protect your family." He paused again, then turned his gaze to the open barn. "Do you have a big freezer? Lots of families have them around these parts."

"We do in the basement. Why?" Krystal said.

Silence that hung in the air. Azura started to laugh.

"What's funny, Mama? I don't get it," Darwin said.

"We need to put Old Gray on ice. She smelled awful before we killed her. Only gonna' get worse, right?"

Adriel nodded. "Maybe if the rest of them think she's not here, they won't come back."

"That's a big maybe. Azura, can you drive the body to the basement? I'll meet you over there and we can drag her down the steps and hopefully get her tucked inside," Bernardo said.

"Hang on. I've got food in there I need to clear out. Give me ten minutes," Krystal said, then headed to the house and disappeared within the orchard.

🦍 🦍 🦍

Cassie carried armfuls of frozen meat up the stairs from the basement and desperately tried to pack it into the kitchen freezer. After numerous trips, the freezer was just about full and she was worried that a good portion of the food would go to waste.

Krystal followed after her, arms loaded with frozen hot dogs, buns, and other goods. "I guess maybe we can barbecue tonight. I'll let these defrost on the counter. There's not much more, sweetie. Thank you for helping me."

Cassie took the ChatBoy out of her pocket and placed it on the kitchen table, which was covered in boxes of frozen Ellio's pizza, ground beef, chicken breast, and more. "I'll go get the rest," she said, heading down the stairs into the basement.

Once into the darkness, she opened the commercial chest freezer and stretched deep into it to gather the rest of the frozen food. Covered in white frost and hard as granite, she had no idea what she liberated from the bottom of the freezer, but it was likely too big to store anywhere else. She placed the frozen food on the steps, then turned to the cellar doors leading outside and unlocked them. The truck rolled up slowly, and she imagined Old Gray's body swaying like clothes on a line, blood still dripping from its corpse. The thought made Cassie shudder.

Suddenly, gunfire. From upstairs. Cassie jumped and turned back to the steps leading up into the kitchen. It hit her. *My tape recorder!*

Charging back upstairs, she found Krystal sitting at the kitchen table, the ChatBoy replaying the audio of the previous night's activity. Azura yelling, Krystal's rapid shots. Bernardo's rifle. Darwin speaking softly to himself in Spanish. Cassie pleading with him to get down and hide. The dogs barking. All of it added up to the sounds of complete anarchy. Distant roars of creatures in the woods, then closer, in the orchard. The last sounds of Old Gray as she died, stumbling toward the woods.

"Cassie ..." Krystal said, clicking the tape off. "I ... I'm so sorry."

"Mom, why?" Cassie stepped to the counter and placed the last bit of frozen food down.

"That sounded so horrible. You and Darwin. You were both so scared."

"We were fine," Cassie said. She leaned over and wrapped her arms around her mom. "Everything was okay."

Krystal shook her head. "We need to get the two of you out of here. At least until we know it's safe. I'll talk to your father, and we'll figure something out. Maybe you can go stay with grandma and grandpa on Long Island for the rest of the summer."

"Mom, no!"

"Cassie, it isn't safe for you to be here. I can't believe I didn't see it sooner. I'm such a bad mother," Krystal said, tears stuck halfway down her cheeks.

Cassie stared into Krystal's eyes. She wrapped her arms around her mom again and hugged her, hard. "I'm not going anywhere, Mom. This is my home, too."

🦍 🦍 🦍

Krystal and Cassie stood in the backyard as Azura, Adriel, and Bernardo carried the body of Old Gray down into the basement. Darwin studied the tree line, eyes bouncing from tree to tree, fingers gripping the charm around his neck.

"What's wrong?" Cassie asked as the three adults struggled to carry the enormous, hairy creature down the steps. Krystal joined them, holding the cellar door open and barking advice on navigating the steps.

"What if they're watching right now? They've been in the woods and mountains for ages. No one's really seen them. They could be there now."

Cassie heard birdsong in the distance. "You hear that, right?" Darwin nodded.

"Remember in the woods? When we didn't hear anything? No birds. Not even a squirrel?"

"Yeah?" Darwin's eyes remained on the forest.

"There's nothing else around when they're around. The birds are chirping. They're not here. Or if they are, they're so far away that they can't see us." She placed a hand on Darwin's shoulder. "It's okay."

He nodded. Cassie hoped her words alleviated his concern. But Darwin didn't turn away from the woods. Fear of the creatures clouded his mind, and it wouldn't be easy to make it go away.

"Come down into the basement," Cassie said. "We should see if they can fit it in there."

The boy nodded as Cassie led him toward the steps, where a light blood trail captured the progress of Old Gray to her new home. Cassie grabbed a roll of heavy-duty paper towels to soak up the blood. She noticed it was thick, almost black, and stuck to the wood like honey. Darwin took half the roll to the top of the steps.

"Do you have a hose?" Darwin asked.

Cassie nodded, abandoned her task for a moment, and walked to the side of the house where she unspooled the hose. She carried it back to Darwin and shivered as the wind from the mountain whisked away the sun's warmth.

"Is it ever gonna' feel like summer?" Cassie asked, tucking herself into her hoodie.

"Where's the jacket I gave you?"

"I left it in my brother's room."

"You could've come in and got it," Darwin said, turning the hose on and spraying the blood away on the grass.

"Mom said I wasn't allowed to go into the room. She told me I had to 'act like a lady' or whatever," Cassie mumbled, turning to hide her discomfort.

"Oh my God, yuck."

"I know, right?"

"Well, I can get it for you once I'm done here."

"That's okay. Why are you spraying down the truck?"

"Well, if they can smell their own, they may think Old Gray's on the truck, so it makes sense to clean it a little bit, at least so they don't pick up the scent. Same with the grass," the boy said, blasting the red-black muck out of the back of the truck and off its rear fender.

Smart.

Bernardo emerged from the cellar, holding his lower back. "Darwin, you don't have to do that. I'll spray it down."

"Almost done, Mr. Albero," Darwin called.

"Darwin, you can call me 'Nardo,' don't be too formal. You're dating my daughter, after all. We're almost family!"

"Dad! Gross!" Cassie shouted, giving him a playful shove.

"Your mama told me what she said at the kitchen table," Bernardo said quietly. "She's not wrong, you know?"

"I don't wanna' go anywhere. I wanna' stay here. This is my home."

Bernardo put his arm around her and pulled her to his hip. "I know, *Cucciola*. I think maybe you and Darwin stay in your rooms tonight. I'm going to camp out with Adriel and his friends."

Cassie looked up at her dad. "Maybe Mom should be the one camped out."

"You little stinker," he said, tickling Cassie until she dropped to the dirt. Darwin watched from the back of the truck, laughing as Cassie collapsed in a heap under her dad's onslaught.

Cassie sat on the porch at the guest house while Darwin and Azura worked on one of the cars parked in the driveway. Azura moved quickly, floating from section to section of the car, its front end up on a series of jacks as the woman moved from under the car to the hood and back. Darwin kept Azura's tools organized and cleaned the components she pulled from under the vehicle.

"You're not scared to stay in the house by yourself?" Cassie asked from the porch, opening a bottle of Mountain Dew and taking a sip.

Azura chuckled. "No, sweetie. I'm going to post up on the upstairs porch tonight. I have a tent. I have a cordless phone. I have my rifle. I'm never alone with all that."

"Why are you camping outside, Mama?" Darwin asked.

"Adriel's friends are all hunters. Deer mostly. That's what these men like to go after up here." Azura wiped her face with a black-streaked towel. "Do you think a bunch of old Indians and white men who spent their lives hunting something that can't fight back will stand a chance against one of those things?"

"You and Cassie's mom did pretty well last night."

"That's true, *hijo*. But they sent her to die. They knew we'd probably kill her."

"What do you mean?" Cassie asked, abandoning the porch.

"Remember how I said she was a distraction? She was older. Maybe near the end of her life already. The other ones come in while we're distracted. May have even been *her* idea. Who knows?"

"The big one. Big Red. He's the leader," Cassie said quietly.

"How do you know?" Darwin asked.

"He's the biggest. Law of the animal kingdom. The biggest, the nastiest. That's usually the alpha," Cassie explained.

Azura nodded. "Your papa hit him last night, right?"

"Yeah. On your porch here."

"Then this *alpha* is injured. May even be dead," Azura said, handing a wrench to Darwin. The boy cleaned it quickly, then tucked it into his mother's toolbox, a disorganized hodgepodge of tools, none of them matching, all of them looking old and well-used. "That means there might be one less to worry about."

Somehow, deep down, Cassie didn't think so. She remembered how the creature lumbered off into the night after being shot. She thought of how Big Red held his back like her dad after carrying something heavy. Being shot was more of an inconvenience, and Big Red was still dangerous.

"I hope you're right," Cassie said quietly, turning her attention to the forest and the mountains. A light mist huddled around the treetops.

No birds. No sound at all beyond the wind bristling through the pines.

CHAPTER TEN

There was tension in the air that night. Adriel had called two of his hunting buddies, but neither could make it to the orchard that night, so Bernardo sat with him in the tent, the flaps open, watching the woods. Azura stayed awake by smoking cigarettes and drinking an entire pot of coffee. She patrolled the area of the forest nearest the guest house. Cassie watched her from the shadows of the orchard and saw Azura raise her rifle to her eye on more than one occasion, as if she saw something deep in the dark gloom of the woods. Each time, she'd shake her head and rest the rifle on the railing and take a deep puff of her cigarette.

Krystal sat on the front porch of the main house, rifle beside her. Like Azura, she drank coffee to keep herself awake and listened for any sign of trouble from the woods, the barn, or the basement. Cassie did her best to stay awake with her, Darwin, too, but eventually exhaustion won out and the kids made their way upstairs, parting at the top of the steps after saying good-night.

As Cassie stared at the blinds blowing lightly in the wind. It seemed colder, even as summer went on. By now, the window on the opposite end of the room would have the air conditioner in it and would be cranking, but not this year. The chill that hung in the air had permeated her bones and seemed to linger with Cassie wherever she went. She was a skinny kid to begin with, so staving off the chill became routine.

By morning, Cassie was freezing. The smell of bacon wafted from downstairs and she rose slowly, burrowing into the heavy blankets. *It's nearly the fourth of July,* she thought, feeling the frustration of the weather on her as her lips quivered in the cold. A few degrees colder and she would see her breath.

She grabbed another hoodie, threw it on, then slipped into Darwin's Starter jacket, a thick pair of sweatpants, and heavy winter socks. She then took her hair dryer and flipped it on, running it up and down her legs and back to warm herself up.

Eventually, she headed downstairs, but not before peeking into Morgan's room. Empty. The bed was made. It looked like no one had been in the room at all. The only hint was Darwin's suitcase at the foot of the bed, neatly tucked against the wall.

In the kitchen, Cassie jumped when she came face to face with a police officer leaning against the counter, a cup of coffee in his hand. Young and tall, but with a terrible, thin mustache that made him look like a cartoon villain. Cassie read his name tag, fastened directly below his badge: *Richardson.*

"Whoa," Richardson said, raising his hands in mock-surrender. "Sorry, didn't mean to scare ya'."

"*Cucciola*, this is Officer Richardson, one of Lakeside's finest," Bernardo called from the back door of the kitchen. He was carrying a large duffel bag into the house. "He's one of Adriel's hunter friends."

"What's going on?" Cassie asked above the bustle of activity in the kitchen. Azura and Krystal stood at the stove, cooking breakfast and making coffee. Darwin sat at the table, eating bacon and pancakes stacked high on a plate at the center of the table.

"Oh, you're Cassandra, I've heard a lot about you from this guy," Richardson said, gesturing to Darwin. "You don't have to be afraid of the uniform. I just got off duty and thought I'd come by and check the place out."

Cassie looked nervously at Darwin, then at Azura.

"I know what you're thinking," Richardson said, kneeling down and looking Cassie in the eye. "The Lakeside Police Department aren't in the business of breaking up families or deporting anybody. I promise. *Serve and Protect.* That's the motto."

Cassie smiled. "Okay," she said, extending her hand. Richardson shook it.

"Plus, who'd fix my Geo if Azura got sent out of here? She fixes half of the Lakeside PD's rides. We'd be outta' luck," Richardson laughed, taking a swig of the coffee.

Adriel stepped into the kitchen. His leg was bandaged and there was red on the knee.

"What happened?" Cassie asked.

Adriel and Bernardo shared a look. Cassie looked toward Krystal, who shook her head and returned to the stove. Azura placed another plateful of pancakes down on the table and poured another cup of coffee.

"After breakfast," Bernardo said, finally.

🦍 🦍 🦍

After breakfast, the group migrated to the porch, taking coffee and orange juice with them.

"We were camped out last night," Adriel began. Bernardo sat beside him, his head low. "'Nardo and I had dozed off maybe around two or three in the morning?"

"Probably around then, yeah."

"When we finally shut our eyes, it was like they knew. Like they were waiting for it."

Cassie's eyes went wide. *How could we not hear them?* she thought, feeling annoyed and scared.

"They came in along the perimeter. All three of them together, just kinda' moving along the edge of the property," Adriel said. "Hiding in the trees. I only know this because I woke up and heard the rustling of branches. I did my best to stay still and just shift my head so I could see them, you know?"

Darwin nodded absently, hanging on every word.

"So, they were near you two?" Officer Richardson asked. "They hung close to you two? Why?"

"Maybe because we fell asleep?" Bernardo asked.

"No," Adriel said. "They know. I'm old. You're not a great shot, you said it yourself. They breach the property line near Azura, they're gonna get tore up by rifle fire."

Azura lit a cigarette and blew a puff of smoke. "God damn right." She offered one to Krystal, who declined at first, then at Azura's insistence, took one and sparked it up.

"I woke up then and moved slowly, pulling myself from the tent. When I got out completely, I saw one. I assume it was the female for, well, *obvious* reasons." Adriel said, then paused to clear his throat. "Her eyes were glowing. Yellow at first in the darkness of the woods, then I noticed a deeper, almost reddish hue to them."

"Like Big Red," Darwin said. "The big one's eyes are red, too."

Adriel nodded. "Could be a tactic. Animals, when feeling threatened, often have different ways to display their feelings. Maybe these things' eyes change color."

"Like a cat?" Officer Richardson asked. "I have a cat at home, Chloe, her eyes are amber-colored, but in the dark, they look green or sometimes a sharp yellow."

"Eyeshine. That's pretty normal. I think Adriel's describing the eyes literally changing color. I assume there was no light?" Azura said.

Adriel shook his head. "Only the moonlight."

"So, these things can change their eye color. Red meaning danger. A color that doesn't always appear in nature. Something unnatural would scare a potential predator," Azura said.

"I've never seen anything like it. I've seen bear rear up on hind legs, I've seen elk charge with their heads down. Nothing like this," Adriel said.

Officer Richardson added, "Same. I hunted cougars in South Dakota a couple of years back. Stayed low and charged. Made a hell of a noise. But that was the scariest I'd ever seen. Watching something's eyes change, though … that's frightening stuff."

"What happened to your leg?" Cassie asked, pointing at Adriel's bandage.

The old man smirked. "Well, I started toward her. I'm not sure what I was thinking, and truthfully, I didn't feel like myself. It was like I was hypnotized or something. I dunno." He leaned back in the rocking chair and sighed. "Anyway, I followed her along the perimeter of the property. She just kinda led me along the tree line. I was maybe ten feet from her. She never bluffed. Never charged. Nothing."

Adriel rubbed his knee absently. Cassie could tell the old man was hurting.

"Do you want some Tylenol or something?" Krystal asked.

"I'll be fine. Anyway, she led me to that long hole in the ground you got over there. I took a tumble and cut my leg pretty good. It's not a big deal, just a limp is all."

"You fell in The Pit?" Darwin asked, amazed.

The old man chuckled. "I guess so. That's when I saw the other two disappearing into the woods. They had their arms full of apples and peaches." Adriel paused. He turned to Bernardo. "I'm sorry, 'Nardo. I didn't have my piece, otherwise, I could've maybe scared them off."

"I'm just glad you're okay," Bernardo said, patting the old man on the back. He turned to his wife, "We need to fill that thing in, baby, someone's gonna break their neck falling into it."

"Once we get the monsters off our property, 'Nardo," Krystal said, pecking him in the cheek. They shared a smirk, and he kissed her again.

"Well Adriel, Benjamin is in Colorado for the month, so he can't be here. But, I have off for the next couple of days. I could maybe camp out with you and help keep an eye on the orchard," Officer Richardson said.

"Thank you. Would that be alright with you folks?"

"You stay a few nights here and kill these things, I'll put a Hemi in that stupid little Geo of yours," Azura said, slapping Officer Richardson on the back.

"Deal," he said, shaking her hand.

Cassie felt good. She felt hopeful. Having a policeman in the orchard, one experienced with hunting, was a huge positive to her and what remained of her summer.

"*Cucciola*, maybe you and Darwin can help with gathering as much ripe fruit as you can?"

Cassie rolled her eyes. "Aww, Dad ..."

"I know, I know, with all the excitement going on, you don't wanna do any work," Bernardo laughed. "But we need you to run the stand and sell some stuff, otherwise ..."

He trailed off. The gravity of the situation hit him and Krystal put her hand on his back, rubbing in small circles. Cassie thought of the conversation at the dinner table what seemed like ages ago. Bernardo talking about the bills piling up. The cold snap. The orchard's output being lower than usual.

"Can you two help out?" Bernardo asked again.

"Of course they can," Azura said. "Darwin, you be a good boy and help Mr. Albero in the orchard today."

"Happy to!" Darwin said with a big smile.

🐾 🐾 🐾

Cassie and Darwin walked the rows, gathering as much ripe fruit as they could. Despite the creatures' theft the past few nights, they were still able to fill their baskets to brimming, taking frequent trips to the farm stand at the edge of the property to resupply Bernardo as he waited for them to finish.

Citiots were in full swing, driving up quickly and scouring the meager offerings of apples and peaches available at the usually overstocked Albero Orchard Farm Stand. Bernardo bustled about, doing his best to help each customer, but to Cassie, he looked like a chicken with his head cut off.

Jellybean, Frick, and Frack escorted the kids to the farm stand and back. Cassie wondered if Jellybean had heard anything the night before. If so, why didn't he bark to wake her up? But Adriel's camp was a fair distance away from the main house, and even the dog's sharp senses had limits.

Darwin looked exhausted as they hauled a final bushel of apples and peaches to the stand. The early morning crowd had given way to the lighter afternoon visitors, and Bernardo was finally able to take a break. The stock from the night before, combined with the resupply that morning, was all but sold out, so this last huge basket of fruit would have to carry the farm stand for the rest of the day.

"Cassandra, I need you two to take over here," Bernardo said. "I need to check in with Adriel and Officer Richardson at the campsite."

"Okay, Dad," Cassie said. She had hoped to get a shower in and scrub the dirt of the orchard off, but that was off the table now. Exhausted, legs like overcooked spaghetti, she sat on a stool possibly older than Adriel and manned a cash register about the same age. Customers filled canvas bags with apples and peaches as part of the Albero Orchard's *Fill a bag with fresh fruit - $25* promotion they ran at the start of every season.

Darwin walked around, filling gaps as customers took apples and peaches. Cassie liked watching Darwin move. He was fast and slick like a cat, darting between customers and placing new stock down without being noticed. Once finished, he walked over to the register and leaned against the counter.

"I really love working in the orchard," he said, squinting into the distance, the sun in his eyes. "It's cold and all, but it's fun."

Cassie nodded. "I'm freezing, even with the jacket. But yeah, it *is* kinda fun. And we get to hang out, so that's cool too."

He turned and smiled at her. "That's my favorite part, actually."

🦍 🦍 🦍

Around four in the afternoon, Cassie began to close down the stand. She and Darwin gathered the last of the fruit, placed it in large baskets and tucked them beside a large refrigerator containing the last of the preserves Krystal had made prior to the attacks. Cassie then gathered the money from the register, carefully counting and placing it in a black metal lockbox stored under the counter. Then she finished locking up the stand, lowering the wooden shutters and fastening them in place with a deadbolt.

"Ready to head back?" Darwin asked. "Need me to carry anything?"

"I'm okay," she said. They walked in silence, enjoying the explosion of colors as the sun fell behind the Dunderberg mountains. In the orchard, they paused to examine the budding fruit. Cassie mentioned it might be a day or two before anything else was ready to be harvested in that section.

"It's cool you know that," Darwin said. Cassie thought he seemed nervous. Distant. *Weird.*

"You okay?"

He shrugged. "Almost dark. They've come here the past couple of nights. Late. I'm just a little freaked out, I guess."

"Me too. It's okay to be scared, right?"

He nodded. Around them, lightning bugs began sparking to life. They radiated green, then faded into the growing darkness as the sun bathed the orchard in orange-purple light.

This felt like the first hint of summer. Lightning bugs were harbingers of the warmth and excitement of summer to come. Cassie felt more relaxed than she had in a long time. The monsters from the woods were cast from her mind. The constant worry she felt for Morgan evaporated.

She surprised Darwin by kissing him on the cheek. He jolted, nervous from the unexpected affection.

"Sorry," she said. "I hope that's okay."

He nodded slowly. Even in the fading light, she could see he was blushing. "Yeah. It's okay."

With the lockbox still clutched to her chest, Cassie took Darwin's hand, and they continued through the orchard with lightning bugs and the sounds of a summer night to carry them.

CHAPTER ELEVEN

At the main house, Cassie and Darwin poured glasses of iced tea and sat at the kitchen table. Krystal, Officer Richardson and Adriel were down in the basement inspecting the body of Old Gray, still in the freezer. As much as Cassie wanted to join them, she was tired and in need of a shower.

She had finished her iced tea and was halfway up the steps when the phone rang. With a sigh, Cassie trudged down the steps and picked the phone up off the receiver. "Hul-lo?"

Static on the other end greeted her, then after a moment of silence. "Hello? Kiddo?"

It was Morgan.

"Oh my god! Morgan!" Cassie shouted.

Her brother laughed at her outburst. There was a two-second delay between Cassie speaking and her brother hearing. Still, the familiar, comforting sound of her brother's voice was impossible to describe. Her eyes began to well, and she held the phone close, as if Morgan could somehow reach through and hug her.

"I miss you. We all do."

"I miss you guys, too. What's new?" Morgan asked after the delay.

Cassie searched for words to adequately describe the events around the property but failed. For a moment she could only focus on the static over the line, then said, "Nothing really. Same old."

Cassie's mom charged up the stairs. At the basement door, she turned and spotted Cassie on the phone. "Is that Morgan?"

She nodded excitedly and handed the phone to Krystal.

"Baby boy?" Krystal almost-whispered into the phone.

Cassie turned to Darwin. "That's my brother on the phone!"

Darwin smiled. He finished his iced tea and rose from the table. "I'm gonna go get showered and changed back at the guest house. Check in on Mom."

Cassie gave him another, more confident, peck on the cheek before he headed out the door. As Cassie turned back toward the phone, she caught her mother's glare. "Let me talk to him again," she said, hand outstretched.

Krystal held the phone from her ear and hit "Speaker". "You're on with me and your sister, baby boy."

"Hey kiddo," Morgan said after a couple of seconds of silence. "I was just telling Mom that I'm sorry I haven't called. We've been, well, kinda busy here."

"We just miss you is all," Cassie said.

"Where's Dad?" Morgan asked.

"He's taking care of some stuff with the orchard," Krystal mumbled. Cassie knew her mom was looking for an adequate lie and that was the best she could come up with. "He might pop in in a second."

"Okay, cool. Cassie, you taking care of the folks?" Morgan asked between bursts of static.

"Of course! When are you coming home?"

"Not sure, kiddo. Depends on if Saddam is gonna stop the nonsense or not." There was a muffled noise in the background of the call, someone talking to either Morgan or another soldier.

Krystal smirked. "Baby boy, everything okay? Can we send you anything?"

"Naw, Ma. I'll call again when we're back in Saudi Arabia," Morgan said. "I have to go now."

"Wait! There's something we—" Krystal began.

"Love ya, Ma! Love ya, Cassie!" Morgan said, cutting his mother off between interjections of static and silence.

"Love you, too," Cassie said in a small, still voice.

The line went dead. Cassie and her mom stood in silence until finally, Krystal placed the receiver back on the hook, uncoiling the spiral phone cable as she hung it up.

"Sounds busy," Krystal said quietly, looking at Cassie. "You okay?"

"Should we have told him what's going on? Like, should we have told him right away?"

"I think it would make him worry more. He doesn't need what's happening here rattling around in his head while he's over there. It's for the best, I guess."

Cassie thought it over. The last thing Morgan needed to hear about were monsters in the woods around the orchard causing trouble. Killing dogs. Scaring his family. *What could he do? It's not like he could just fly home and save the day.* Cassie sighed and placed the tea glasses in the sink, giving them a quick rinse in the process.

"I'm gonna go take a shower," Cassie said, starting back up the steps. "Do you need me to do anything before you guys settle in for the night?"

Krystal froze her daughter in place with a look. "Don't think I didn't see the little kiss you gave that boy."

"Aw, Mom, stoooop!" Cassie groaned, running up the stairs and disappearing into the bathroom.

🦍 🦍 🦍

That night, Cassie, Krystal, Bernardo, Officer Richardson (who was in normal clothes and looking very different from when he was in uniform), Adriel, and Azura sat around a campfire on the edge of the orchard's property line. Darwin sat beside Azura, eating his third hot dog of the night and drinking a Mountain Dew.

Bernardo listened intently as Officer Richardson told stories of hunting a variety of creatures across the United States. The weapon he unpacked and put together was the real deal. Adriel commented that it was *a little too flashy* for his tastes, but Officer Richardson explained that the Belgian-produced gun was more of an assault rifle than a traditional rifle. Sleek and black, with a short muzzle, he referred to the weapon as *Nancy*.

"Named her after Nancy Sinatra," he said, smiling proudly, turning the gun to catch the light of the campfire.

Azura smiled. "We had a few of those in the revolution. Not many. Never fired one m'self."

Officer Richardson offered it to her. "By all means, try it out. Feel the weight."

Azura held the gun in her hands. She flipped it around, checked the safety a second time and hoisted it high, aiming down the rail. She passed it back to Officer Richardson. "What kind of ammo?"

Officer Richardson shifted in his lawn chair. "Well, truth be told," he said, leaning forward, the shadows from the campfire dancing on his face. "I have it loaded with hollow points. Not exactly street legal."

"What's a hollow point?" Darwin asked.

"Dum dum bullets. They sorta *open up* when they hit something," Azura said. "Not legal around here."

Officer Richardson shook his head. "Staties got them off a group of cartel thugs heading up north. Officially, they've been destroyed. Unofficially, I may have taken them all for myself."

"Bullets that expand? Sounds dangerous," Krystal said.

Words droned together as Cassie turned her attention to the woods. Deep in the shadows, a pair of glowing yellow eyes stared back at her. The conversation grew further muddled as her adrenaline surged. But when she tried to focus on the eyes, they vanished. There was no telltale stench, and she could hear bugs buzzing in the orchard and a wayward owl hooting in the treetops.

Jellybean stirred, his ears flicking at the sound of the owl. She thought about Frick and Frack patrolling the main house. Cassie wondered if they heard anything. Were the monsters already ransacking the basement as they sat around a campfire talking about bullets and guns and nonsense.

"That thing in the basement is really something else. I hope I get to see a live one," Officer Richardson said.

"No, you don't," Cassie said, her voice both stoic and fearful.

"Cassandra!" Bernardo said. "Sorry, Officer. These things are ... very different. Scary. Cassie got close to one on her own. It, uh, killed one of the dogs."

"I'm really sorry," Officer Richardson said in a practiced but genuine way.

Adriel yawned. He opened the top of a Thermos and took a hearty swig. *Strong coffee,* he called it. Brewed earlier that evening, Adriel had been sipping all night to not repeat the night before. "We better take our positions. I'll work on putting out this fire," he said.

Bernardo headed toward the tents. The small camp Adriel had put together the night before had expanded with Officer Richardson's equipment. There was a second tent, along with a smaller pop-up that housed a table and two large coolers loaded with food and drinks. The officer kept his additional supplies there, including a walkie-talkie (the other two were with Krystal and Azura respectively), a camcorder, two hunting knives, a compass, and two first aid kits.

"Seems like a lot for only a couple of nights," Darwin said.

"You never know. Better safe than sorry," Officer Richardson said.

Adriel approached Bernardo. Cassie couldn't make out the words exchanged, but her dad was obviously upset. Eventually, Bernardo shook his head, placed his sleeping bag down on the table of supplies, and nodded in an attempt to end the conversation rather than from agreement.

Adriel placed his hand on Bernardo's shoulder and said something else. Cassie thought it was *I'm sorry*, but she couldn't hear above the commotion of the others gathering their supplies and heading to their posts.

🦍 🦍 🦍

Bernardo stood on the front porch, revolver in his holster as he leaned against the railing. Adriel had given him the weapon because it had better stopping power than the Krystal's pistol.

Bernardo sipped from a steaming cup of coffee and surveyed the orchard. Every once in a while, he'd glance over toward the guest house. Cassie could just barely make out Azura on the upstairs back porch. She just had to look for the dance of smoke in the air. None of the lights in the guest house were on, and every once in a while, Cassie saw Azura raise the rifle to her eye, taking a quick peek through the recently added scope (a gift from Adriel after a quick stop at the store).

In the living room, Darwin watched the news. War machines firing rockets in the Middle East. Night-vision footage of a desert war Cassie knew her brother was becoming acquainted with.

Rifle slung over her shoulder, Krystal paced the length of the back porch. She kept her eyes glued to the forest and cradled the walkie-talkie in her hand. Every once in a while, the walkie crackled to life. Officer Richardson mentioned it was important to stay in contact with one another. Cassie heard her dad on the front porch scoff at the intrusion while Krystal checked in with Adriel and Officer Richardson, then Azura. Cassie rationalized that Bernardo was feeling left out, muttering in Italian under his breath.

"We had a good day today at the stand," Cassie said, trying to distract her dad.

He smiled weakly. "That's great, *Cucciola*."

Cassie looked at the revolver tucked in her dad's holster. "That new gun looks cool."

Bernardo smirked. Even in the moonlight, Cassie could see something was wrong. Her dad's face was a blend of annoyance, exhaustion, and sadness. "No gun is *cool*, Cassandra."

Krystal's walkie squawked to life. Bernardo's head turned slightly, and Cassie turned with him to listen. Darwin muted the television.

"Movement in the tree line," Officer Richardson said over the walkie.

Cassie held her breath and listened. No owls. No bugs. In the orchard, she couldn't see the slightest hint of lightning bugs dancing among the trees. She took a tentative step off the porch and again searched for meaning in shadows.

"Azura, can you see anything from where you are?" Officer Richardson asked over the radio. "Maybe ten feet into the brush?"

Cassie turned toward the guest house as Azura raised the rifle to her eye. She lowered the rifle and raised the walkie-talkie to her mouth. "Negative. I don't see anything."

"Hang on," Krystal said into the walkie. Bernardo turned his attention to his wife. She stood, framed in the open doorway to the back porch. "I think I see something ..."

A chorus of *whoops* erupted from the forest. Though Cassie was confused by the noise, she could make out three distinct voices. One deeper, almost a snarl. Another louder, piercing and with a sharpness Cassie hadn't heard before. A third mingled with the others, sounding like a person doing an impression of an owl. The dominant sounds were inhuman, far more animalistic. The third voice held a steadier register and could have been Adriel or her dad.

Cassie stepped up onto the porch and pulled the ChatBoy from her pocket. She hit RECORD and held the device up, the cacophony of calls unceasing. The tempo increased, building almost to a frenzy. Then there was nothing. The silence was more frightening than the noise. As if the monsters had been arguing about the next action and a decision was made.

The walkie squawked to life, making Krystal, Darwin and Cassie jump. "What do you see, Krystal?" Azura asked.

Cassie stepped into the house and started toward the back door. Bernardo grabbed her by the shoulder before she reached it. He knelt to her eye level. "You and Darwin. Upstairs now."

Darwin went first and Cassie followed. They ran to the row of windows overlooking the backyard in her parents' bedroom. Krystal had stepped off the porch, her rifle at the ready. Bernardo joined her after, revolver in his hand.

"I don't see anything now," Krystal said into the radio.

Fa-kwoom! Without warning, the entire house rattled from the force of something slamming against it. This was followed shortly after by a hail of smaller impacts along the eastern side of the house. Darwin struggled to see in the direction of the noise, but Cassie kept her eyes on her parents, who ducked for cover, holding their hands above their heads and sprinting toward the back door of the house.

The barrage intensified with glass shattering and wood cracking from impacts Cassie did not understand. Was it a chain?

"The basement!" Cassie screamed.

"*Cucciola*? You alright? Darwin?" Bernardo shouted from downstairs. Cassie ran to the doorway of her parents' bedroom and looked down the steps at her dad. There was blood on his head, a tiny trail from his forehead to his right cheek.

"They're trying to get into the basement!" Cassie screamed.

Bernardo slammed the front door and locked it. The walkie-talkie fizzed and crackled, Azura shouting something Cassie couldn't make out over the noise of some still unidentified thing slamming into the house.

Krystal appeared at the bottom of the steps. "Stay upstairs! No matter what you hear, don't come down into the basement!"

Krystal grabbed Bernardo and they disappeared beneath the landing of the stairs, heading back toward the basement. Cassie couldn't move. Her fingers tapped the wooden railing. Darwin joined her and held his ears, jumping as glass shattered and more impacts rattled the house.

"What's happening?" Darwin asked. He sounded desperate. Scared.

Cassie opened her mouth to answer, but before she could, gunshots echoed from the basement. Cassie charged down the stairs, leaping over the last two steps and tearing hard and fast down the hallway toward the kitchen. Once there, she flung the basement door open.

As she crept down the steps, she noticed the sound of whatever had been hitting the house had ceased. At the bottom, she saw Bernardo holding onto the cellar doors, his entire body struggling against whatever was trying to pull the doors open from the outside. Krystal aimed her rifle through a large hole in the wooden door and pulled the trigger again, the sound of the gunfire deafening in the small basement. Cassie covered her ears as the creature on the other side of the cellar door let loose an animal cry just louder than the ringing in her ears.

Ruuuuughghhhhraaaaa! The bellow made Cassie's knees weak. She'd never before heard an expression of pain like that in the real world. Even the other night, when Old Gray was being shot, she did so in near silence. Cassie was reminded of the T-Rex in *King Kong* that screamed while Kong broke its jaw and beat it to death on Skull Island. Ice water trickled down Cassie's spine.

Krystal reared back as the tension on the door from the other side let up. Bernardo held firm, his knuckles turning white. From a distance, the sound of another rifle shot. *Azura*? In the panic, Cassie spotted the walkie-talkie on the floor beside Bernardo. Careful not to break her father's concentration, she kneeled and retrieved it.

"Cassie to Adriel," she said softly.

"Cassandra, go upstairs!" Bernardo screamed, the door giving a hard lurch, before crashing back down, throwing him onto his back. The door struggled against the chains placed there after Old Gray was locked in the freezer.

The doors stretched outward, wooden hinges struggling to remain in place. Krystal slipped the rifle through a different hole in the cellar door and fired again, the sound reverberating off the walls of the basement. Bernardo scrambled to his feet and pulled the revolver from his holster, pressing the barrel to another hole in the door and firing off three rapid shots.

Cassie heard voices nearby. *Adriel! Officer Richardson! The cavalry!* Whatever was pulling on the door let it go, and it slammed back down, the chain rattling hard. Cassie heard heavy footsteps running away, growing softer and softer as the assailant made a hasty escape toward the tree line along the backyard.

Cassie passed the walkie-talkie back to Krystal. She took the ChatBoy out of her pocket and hit STOP to end the recording. Bernardo breathed heavily, his hands bleeding from the friction of holding the metal handles of the door so tightly. Krystal placed her rifle down and walked over to her husband, examining his head wound.

"Let's get you cleaned up," she whispered, leading Bernardo toward the stairs.

He stopped and turned to Cassie. "What were you thinking? I told you to stay upstairs."

"I'm sorry, Daddy, I–"

"This isn't a game, *Cucciola*."

With that, Krystal helped Bernardo up the stairs and into the kitchen. Cassie stood alone in the basement holding the ChatBoy. Quietly, she began to cry.

Later, Cassie learned it was Azura shooting from the distance. To no one's surprise, she was able to tag the monster at the cellar door from the elevated porch not once, but twice. Adriel supposed that meant it was the big one at the cellar door, not the one Cassie saw behind the barn or the other female.

"That noise they made was a distraction. They were trying to get our attention all over the orchard," Officer Richardson said.

Azura nodded. "One was in the woods by me. I could hear it. Couldn't see it, though."

"One by us, too. I think the younger one," Adriel said.

"Impossible. Something was nailing our house with rocks. Broke three windows," Krystal said.

Adriel looked at her. "But there were only four to begin with, yes?"

"We've *seen* four. Could be ten. Could be a hundred," Krystal said.

Bernardo scoffed. "There are four. I think these things can do more than just play tricks on us. Adriel, one of them whammied you last night, right? Made you confused?"

Adriel nodded. Cassie could tell he was thinking about the night before as the old man absently rubbed his injured leg. "That's right."

"Maybe they can make us *think* there's more of them. Do animals do that?" Azura asked.

Officer Richardson answered, "Anything's possible, I guess. Who the heck's ever come into contact like this with these kinds of critters. That big one's been shot how many times now?"

"At least four," Bernardo said, touching the bandage near his hairline.

"Shot four times with a rifle and still standing," Officer Richardson said, shaking his head. "That's really something."

"Their skin is thicker than ours. Almost like your bulletproof vests or somethin'. So, they can take a licking and keep on ticking. They can hypnotize us. They can make so much noise that we think there's an *army* of them beating down our doors. How?" Azura said.

Darwin sat on the end of the porch looking lost in thought. Cassie joined him there and said, "I recorded them again."

"I hate how they sound," Darwin said. "I hope I never hear them again."

Krystal turned to the two kids. "You two should try to get some sleep."

"I think we should be taught to shoot," Cassie said quietly.

"What's that?" Bernardo asked. He took a step toward his daughter. "What'd you say?"

Cassie stood and faced her father. "I know you think it's dangerous, but you should show me how to use the guns. Darwin already knows. Why can't I?"

"Little lady, guns aren't a toy. Your parents are right to keep this stuff from you," Officer Richardson said.

"Keep it from me? It almost ripped the basement doors off. It killed Louise. Broke our windows," Cassie said, her voice rising. "I need to know how to defend myself. It's not fair that Darwin knows and I don't."

Azura approached Cassie and placed her hand on the girl's shoulder. "Darwin only knows because he *had* to know. I never wanted him to learn. But, in the jungle, you do what you have to do. Your parents are doing the best they can."

Cassie nodded. She could feel the frustration waning. She was tired. The adrenaline surge was starting to wear off and she was feeling wiped out. "I know," she finally said. "I'm sorry."

"It's okay, *Cucciola*. Maybe head upstairs and mama and I'll come see you in a bit," Bernardo said.

Cassie nodded. She turned and walked into the house, followed by Darwin.

CHAPTER TWELVE

It must have been their plan all along. The things in the woods. The attack earlier in the night was a "feint," as Morgan would call it.

Cassie learned what a feint was three years prior when she was having trouble with Rose Balchi on the school bus. A girl whose name belied her attitude and outward appearance, Rose was always a bully. A nasty young girl who never gave a correct answer in class and hated anyone who did. Cassie was not afraid of her, usually flying under Rose's radar at school. That is, until Cassie proved adept at climbing the rope in gym class, something Rose couldn't do on account of being thirty pounds overweight.

That afternoon on the bus, Rose let Cassie have it. She threw wad after wad of gum at Cassie, most of it getting stuck in her thick hair. Glowing globs of purple and pinks and greens melted into Cassie's curly black locks. When Cassie asked her to stop,

Rose simply stood, stalked over to her, and slapped her hard across the face. The kids on the bus, most of whom had been laughing at the gum in Cassie's hair, fell silent at the physical escalation.

A rage that had never really been present in Cassie before swelled in her chest. Her cheeks burned and she began to cry. Rose took this as a sign of victory and continued berating her target, mimicking Cassie and calling her a baby among other insults Cassie had forgotten in the past three years.

Morgan met Cassie on the front porch after school. It was their custom. He'd get home before her, make a quick snack, and the two would rush off for an adventure in the woods. They'd explore The Pit or work in the orchard before settling in to do their homework before dinner. When Morgan saw the gum in his little sister's hair and the redness on Cassie's cheek (from being slapped or from crying, he wasn't sure), he led her to the bathroom and wiped her face with a warm hand towel.

While Krystal and Bernardo worked in the orchard, Morgan took Cassie to the kitchen and used ice cubes to freeze the gum in his little sister's hair. He then carefully peeled it from the thick strands, tossing each piece in the garbage while Cassie told him all about the incident and about Rose in general. Morgan listened. He always listened. When Cassie began crying again, Morgan was halfway through pulling the last bit of gum from her dark curls. Once her hair was gum-free, he spun his sister around on the chair and looked her in the eye.

"Go hop in the shower then meet me by The Pit. Be quick about it, kiddo."

Quick was a relative term. Cassie knew that when Morgan told her to *be quick* it really meant to move faster than light. Faster than The Flash. Cassie tore up the steps, hopped in the shower and was out the door, still dripping, in record time. Her hair was clean. She was in fresh clothes and her brother wanted to hang out at The Pit. The evening was promising to be better than the afternoon, and Cassie was curious about what Morgan wanted to show her.

At The Pit, Morgan paced around near the edge. She stepped over slowly and he turned. In a flash, Morgan went to slap Cassie, stopping about five inches from her face. The result was the same. Cassie flinched and ducked from his swipe, landing squarely on her rear end in the dirt.

"Hey, what gives?" Cassie shouted, feeling tears beginning to well up again for the third time that day.

"Kiddo," Morgan said, walking over to her and helping her back up. "I'm gonna show you something to help you deal with that schmuck from school."

"She's bigger than me. I wouldn't stand a chance," Cassie said as she brushed herself off.

"You're right. You won't. Not if you fight fair."

He swung his open right palm at Cassie again, and Cassie didn't flinch. Unfortunately, his left moved faster, checking her in the stomach with the back of his hand. It didn't hurt, but it caught her off guard and made her jump just the same.

"See that?"

"Not really," Cassie said, rubbing her stomach absently.

"I didn't hurt you, right? You were so focused on the hand coming for your face that you never saw my other hand coming for your belly."

"Yeah," Cassie said. She wasn't following his logic. "So what?"

"It's called a feint. You throw a punch with one hand, but really come in with the other. They do it in boxing all the time. The key is to keep your eyes on the other guy's eyes."

Cassie nodded as the lesson began to sink in. "So, you're saying I should go to punch Rose in the face with one hand and hit her in the stomach with the other?"

"Couldn't hurt. Then, when she grabs her stomach, knee her in the face so hard she never messes with you again."

"I don't know," Cassie said, her voice trailing off.

Morgan rolled his eyes. "You want this to keep happening or do you want to handle it like a badass?" He threw another right-handed slap at Cassie and again caught her in the stomach with his left. This time, he didn't hold back. Cassie doubled over, nearly dropping to her knees.

Morgan grabbed the back of her shirt and Cassie saw his Converse sneakers shuffling in the dirt underneath her. She gritted her teeth and prepared for the aforementioned knee to the face.

"Then you do this," Morgan said, lifting his right knee slowly and lightly nudging Cassie's temple. "I'm not going to knee you in the head, dingus. Relax."

He released her and she stood, smoothing her shirt and holding her stomach. "Didn't have to hit me so hard."

"I know. But you need to be ready in case this brat tries it again."

Morgan started back toward the house. Cassie looked down at her sneakers, kicked a rock into The Pit, and turned toward him before he disappeared into the orchard. "What else can you show me?"

Morgan turned around, beaming. He had plenty to show her.

🦍 🦍 🦍

A feint was exactly what the creatures executed. Cassie wondered which was the smartest of the three that were left. Big Red? The mama? *Was 'Big Mama' too on the nose?* Cassie wondered. *And what about the smaller one? What silly name did Darwin have for that one?*

It didn't matter. When the creatures attacked a second time that night, long after the adrenaline of the first attack had worn off and exhaustion had begun to take root, all three creatures breached the property from three separate angles.

Cassie bolted upright in bed at the sound of a rifle firing. *Azura*, Cassie thought. It wasn't really a thought. She knew

Azura would stay awake. The woman was a machine and machines don't sleep. Not after an attack like the one earlier. Jellybean roused, too, and began growling in the darkness of the bedroom.

After that first gunshot, Cassie heard the *whoops* from all directions outside. East closer to the guest house. West closer to the mountains. Even south by the end of the driveway near the orchard's roadside stand. Almost immediately, confusion set in as her parents coordinated their response. Krystal must have fallen asleep on the back porch and Bernardo on the front.

Another round of gunfire, closer to The Pit, near the campsite. Adriel and Officer Richardson. Cassie hoped they could take at least one of the creatures down, but the consistency of gunfire thundering outside the house led Cassie to believe that they weren't landing shots at all and maybe were just firing blindly into the dark.

Cassie heard Darwin scrambling around Morgan's bedroom, with Frick and Frack barking like maniacs. Cassie dressed quickly, throwing on a heavy hoodie, the Starter jacket, a thick pair of jeans and a pair of Airwalks. Something inside Cassie told her she'd need to do some running and the Airwalks were perfect.

"Darwin?" Cassie shouted.

"Cassandra? You okay?"

A *thump* against the house drew Cassie's attention. It wasn't near the cellar door like last time. Instead, this was on the front porch. "Dad!" Cassie screamed as she threw open her bedroom door and charged down the steps. Once there, she heard gunfire coming from the front porch. Flashes of light on the other side let Cassie know that Bernardo was okay, or okay enough to shoot at something. Three shots. A fourth.

Cassie slowly opened the front door. Bernardo stood near the edge of the porch, flashlight carving through shadows. The beam fell on the orchard, on the cars in the driveway, then on the opposite end of the porch. The orchard was bathed in a blanket of fog, the mist descending from the mountains to swallow every acre of land.

"Dad?" Cassie whispered. Jellybean stood beside her, waiting, ears tucked against the side of his head, watching the fruit trees and growling softly.

Bernardo turned, the beam of the flashlight blinding her. She held her hand up to shield her eyes. "*Cucciola*, go back upstairs. They're here ..." he whispered before a large rock cracked Bernardo in the back, downing him quickly. The revolver slipped from his hand and slid into the house, past Cassie, and into the living room.

She rushed to her dad and began tugging on him. The rock had done damage. His shoulder was out of its socket. This had happened to Morgan half a dozen times and she felt a pang of sickness course through her body as she grabbed the flashlight and examined the injury. The flesh bulged in places it shouldn't, and Bernardo groaned in agony as he tried to crawl into the house.

Cassie aimed the flashlight at the orchard and saw, for an instant, the face of one of the creatures. Yellow eyes. Tall. Not Big Red. *Big Mama.* She kept the light on her awhile, staring deep into her focused eyes. They shimmered like stars within the tight flesh on her face surrounded by thick, dark hair. Then the smell hit Cassie like a ton of bricks.

Cassie, as if in a trance, took a step off the porch and headed toward the yellow-eyed creature. Flashlight in hand, Cassie saw it in greater detail as she neared. Seven feet tall. Black-red fur. Thicker on the stomach and legs, but still thick all over its body, which was mostly covered in hair. Steam issued from its wide nose and the space in its mouth where the lips failed to meet, courtesy of two large fangs protruding from the top and bottom of the mouth. No neck. It looked as though the creature wore a hood. Its head rested on a dense mound of muscular flesh.

Closer still, Cassie could hear the creature taking deep breaths, followed by wheezing exhales. It extended a hand and the girl did the same, entranced by the female creature's deep, glowing yellow eyes.

"*Cucciola*, no!" Bernardo cried from the front door. Cassie turned and saw her father, leaning on the doorframe, pistol extended. He squeezed off a round and hit the creature in the side of the neck. Jellybean pounced and began attacking the creature as well. In her trance, Cassie had completely forgotten about the Labrador, and the dog barked and snarled, peppering the towering giant with bites all over its legs and feet as it stumbled around.

Cassie hit the dirt as the creature lumbered, as if confused by what happened. Raising the flashlight, she watched the creature shield its eyes, staring as if in complete disbelief at being shot. A low grumble, followed by more wheezing, escaped the creature's mouth before Bernardo fired off another round. Cassie heard the *whizz* of the bullet zipping past her and the creature.

Gunfire was still going off all around the orchard. Cassie scrambled to her feet and dashed the front porch, slipping past her dad and into the living room. He slammed the door and locked it, struggling with one hand to reload the revolver. His hands shaking, he lost his grip on both the gun and the bullets and they scattered across the floor. Jellybean took position between Bernardo and Cassie, his ears twitching with every noise from outside.

Cassie began gathering the bullets when Darwin joined her, doing the same. He grabbed the revolver and, with a flick of the wrist, the boy activated the cylinder release and emptied the spent shells onto the floor. He then slipped two rounds into the cylinder, then took the other three from Cassie and slipped them in place before turning to Bernardo.

"There's only five here. Do you have another?"

"I didn't take any more before I left the camp before."

Darwin handed the revolver back to Bernardo. Rifle fire out back made them all turn toward the kitchen.

"Mom is out there," Cassie said.

A monstrous *thump* at the front door drew their attention back in that direction. Cassie peered through the window beside the front door but couldn't see anyone on the porch. Then, an arm tore through the glass, grabbing the girl by the hair. Screaming, Cassie reached up and clawed at the creature's hand. It had lifted her two feet off the ground before Bernardo ran over and fired three rounds into the creature's arm.

With a howl, the monster let Cassie go and she dropped to the floor. Wincing, Cassie felt the back of her head and knew she'd be missing a few chunks of hair. She checked her fingers. Bloody.

"Two shots left," Darwin said.

Bernardo looked around. His shoulder bulged unnaturally, and his face was pinched in agony. His head wound had reopened and he was coated in sweat. The cool summer no longer mattered once adrenaline started flowing. Bernardo took deep gulps of air and turned his attention to the back door. A quiet came over the orchard, and Cassie listened for movement around the house.

They heard the walkie-talkie in the back yard squawk a few times. "Adriel to Krystal, do you copy?"

Slowly, Darwin stepped toward the back door in the kitchen and opened it with a creak. Cassie walked over to get a good look, and they were joined by Bernardo, revolver at the ready. The motion sensor light was on, and it bathed the yard in a bright white cone illuminating Krystal's rifle. Next to it, the walkie-talkie. Frick and Frack had slipped outside during the fracas and sniffed the ground around the rifle and walkie. Jellybean paced beside Cassie, tense and ready for action.

"Krystal? Baby?" Bernardo said softly, stepping off the porch into the mist.

"Mom?" Cassie called, her voice anxious and trembling. Her mind went to the worst possible place. They had taken her mother. Another feint. Attack the front of the house. Distract everyone inside. Attack near the guest house. Draw everyone's attention all over and pick the humans off one by one.

The walkie-talkie crackled with static, and Bernardo picked it up.

"Krystal isn't here," he said into the handset.

Another round of gunfire, this time from Adriel's camp. Cassie thought it sounded like the footage of the war in Iraq, the flashes of light in the distance and the *pop-pop-pop* of Officer Richardson's assault rifle filled the young girl with terror. Darwin stepped out onto the porch and turned toward the guest house.

"Mama ..." he said, before sprinting off through the orchard toward the guest house.

"Darwin, no!" Cassie shouted. He froze in the orchard and turned back to her.

"But my mom!" he screamed.

"Stay here!" Bernardo shouted.

He turned back to his daughter and pulled her close. "Listen to me," he began. He placed the revolver in her hands. "Take this and go to the top of the stairs. If you see anything taller than me or Officer Richardson, you pull the trigger. Like in the movies, okay?"

Cassie stared into her dad's eyes. He was desperate. Scared. "What're you going to do?"

He picked up Krystal's rifle. "I'm going to find your mother."

"Please don't leave me," Cassie said, tears forming. Darwin stepped onto the back porch, eyes wide, watching the guest house.

Bernardo took the walkie-talkie and held it up. "Azura, come to the main house. I need you to watch Darwin and Cassandra."

"Copy that," Azura said.

🦍 🦍 🦍

It seemed like hours until Azura arrived, emerging from the orchard with the rifle slung over her shoulder and two pistols tucked in the waistband of her jeans. She took one out and handed it to Darwin without hesitation.

"I won't be long. I'm going to go into the woods to find Krystal," Bernardo said.

Azura shook her head. "You should wait for Adriel. Or the cop. Going in there by yourself is a bad idea."

"It's my *wife*, Azura. Stay with the kids. I'll be back in a bit."

"You're hurt, man," Azura called as Bernardo stalked toward the woods. He paused a moment and slammed his shoulder into a tree, jamming it back into socket.

"Stay with them," Bernardo hissed before disappearing into the woods.

Azura lifted the radio to her lips. "Azura to Adriel. Circle back to the main house and dip into the woods. Bernardo went in after Krystal."

"What?" Adriel shouted over the walkie. "Is he nuts?"

"Obviously. Send the cop back here. We're low on ammo and these things are still out there."

"Copy that," Adriel said, the line hissing static a moment before Azura tucked it into her pocket.

Azura turned to Cassie. "Keep that thing pointed to the ground unless you're looking to shoot someone, okay?"

Cassie nodded. She lowered the revolver to her side.

"These things are big. Aim for their chest. Don't hesitate, either."

The kids nodded and returned to the house. Azura knelt in the doorway and scanned the tree line as Darwin moved to the living room, keeping watch on the front of the house. Cassie placed the revolver on the kitchen table and stood near the door to the basement. Suddenly, she heard a *thud* of something moving underneath them.

"Azura," Cassie said softly. Jellybean scratched at the basement door as Frick and Frack joined her beside the closed door.

The woman entered the kitchen from the back porch. "What's wrong?"

"I think there's something in the basement. I heard something moving down there," Cassie said.

"*Mierda,*" Azura said angrily. She turned to the basement door and opened it slowly. There was definitely something moving around down there. She tried the light switch, but it only cast shadows around the bottom of the stairs leading into the basement proper. "Darwin, watch the back porch for the cop. How many shots you got left in that canon, Cassie?"

"Two, I think."

Azura nodded. She handed the girl the other pistol from her waistband. "Same idea as before. Keep it low. Aim for their chest."

Cassie tucked the revolver into her jeans like Azura and followed the woman down the steps, Jellybean in tow. As they reached the bottom, Azura inched the business-end of the rifle around the corner at the bottom and froze in place.

"*Madre de Dios*," she whispered to the dark. Cassie and Jellybean came up beside her and saw Big Red, ducking low, tearing the freezer open with relative ease. With enormous arms, the creature reached in and started to pull Old Gray from her icy coffin.

Raising the rifle, Azura fired, the sound echoing again in the confined space. She didn't miss, but the round barely did any damage to the mammoth leaning over the freezer. He merely lurched a bit, his back erupting red. He turned, Old Gray's frozen body stiff in his arms. Frick and Frack charged the creature, jumping, biting at his arms and legs.

With a *ruggghhhhhr*, Big Red spun, dropping Old Gray to the hard floor. His head slammed into the low ceiling of the basement, and he floundered around in a daze. Azura raised her rifle again and fired, the shot catching Big Red square in the chest. It punched a hole in him, but one not as large as the one in Old Gray. Big Red recoiled and bellowed, kicking Frick hard across the room.

Cassie knew Frick was dead the second Big Red's foot collided with his small frame. Frack attacked more, tearing into what Cassie imagined was Big Red's Achilles tendon. Jellybean charged as well, targeting the creature's right arm, using its weight to pull the beast down.

Aiming quickly, Azura fired again, this time catching Big Red in the head. In a rage, the monster kicked Jellybean away, then reached down and grabbed Frack by its tail. With his other massive hand, he grabbed Frack by the neck and pulled in opposite directions, tearing the German shepherd in two. An arch of blood and viscera erupted, splashing both Cassie and Azura. Screaming, Cassie raised the pistol and squeezed off multiple rounds. The bullets impacted the wall behind Big Red, as well as a few reaching home in his massive chest. A small section at the top of the creature's head was missing, and Cassie just barely made out the reddish-white skull in the opened wound.

Azura fired again as the creature knelt to retrieve Old Gray. It stumbled around, clearly in a daze from the gunshots and dog bites. Blood from a dozen wounds pooling on the basement floor. It ascended the stairs slowly, and as Azura went to fire her rifle again, she cursed under her breath, realizing she was out of bullets. She grabbed the pistol from Cassie and followed Big Red up the steps, emptying the clip into his back as it lumbered.

Jellybean lay on his side, whimpering softly in the dim light of the basement. Cassie knelt beside him and rubbed behind the dog's ears. "You're gonna be okay," she whispered. "I'll be right back."

More gunfire from outside drew Cassie's attention from the wounded dog. She turned and charged up the steps, following the trail of blood left behind by Big Red. At the top of the stairs, she watched Azura follow the creature across the lawn, pulling the trigger long after the final round had been fired.

"Big tough man, right?" Azura whispered to the stumbling animal. *Click-click-click* of the pistol with every step. Cassie thought the woman had lost her mind.

Officer Richardson appeared, raising his assault rifle and opening fire. Darwin stood beside him and squeezed off multiple rounds from the pistol. Each shot rattled Big Red, but the creature continued onward. He took a few more tentative steps toward the trees before turning, his body riddled with bullets, steam pouring from his mouth and nose.

Cassie stood frozen and watched as the creature buckled, still holding Old Gray.

Officer Richardson stepped closer to Big Red's body. Steam still streamed from the creature's mouth and nose. "It's still alive."

Darwin attempted to approach but was cut off by Azura. She stole the pistol from him, aimed it at the back of Big Red's head, and emptied the rest of the bullets into its enormous skull.

"Not anymore, it's not," she said. In the beam of the motion sensor light, Cassie made out brain and chunks of skull splattered on the lawn.

The sudden static of the walkie-talkie in Azura's hand made everyone jump. "Azura, I've got Bernardo. No sign of Krystal."

"Copy that. We killed the big one."

Static.

"We'll be back soon," Adriel said after a long silence.

"Any sign of Krystal?" Azura asked.

Nothing. Cassie waited, holding her breath for a response, but none came.

"They couldn't have gotten far," Officer Richardson said, turning to Cassie. "They'll find–"

Rughhhhawrrrr! Officer Richardson was bulldozed to the ground by something huge and fast. The other big one. The Mama. Without stopping, she charged through the group, bowling the officer over again before disappearing into the trees. Darwin froze. The creature was within two feet of him and he could've just as easily been knocked to the ground.

The Officer struggled to rise, but collapsed. Cassie and Azura darted over to help when the smaller one from the barn leaped from the shadows and attacked, swinging its long, thin arms wildly. The creature's leathery hand slapped Cassie's face, knocking her onto her back. She rolled away as it rained blows down on Azura. Darwin went for the pistol, but the second he did, the younger one turned toward him.

"Hey!" Cassie screamed, desperate to get the creature's attention.

It turned and Cassie was finally able to get a clear look. He was lean. Awkward in the same way as Darwin with his long limbs. Still growing. Still getting used to his body. One golden eye caught the glow of the motion sensor light as he stalked toward her.

Darwin raised the pistol and pulled the trigger. *Click-click-click-click*. Empty. Cassie remembered how moments ago, Azura poured every shot into the now-dead Big Red's skull. The young one turned toward Darwin and swiped with its long arm, knocking the gun away. He followed with a quick swipe to the left, knocking Darwin to the ground. The way the boy's body crumpled; Cassie imagined every bone in his body exploding like the dynamite used to collapse old mines.

Scrambling to her feet, the young one turned toward her. He snarled and crouched low, bobbing left and right as he moved, more ape than human. Cassie thought he looked like an overgrown chimpanzee. He pummeled gnarled fists down on Azura again and Cassie recoiled at the sound of bone breaking mingled with Azura's cries in both Spanish and English.

"Come on, Ahab," Cassie grunted, holding her side. She struggled to catch her breath as the collision had knocked the wind out of her. "You look like an asshole pirate with one eye."

Cassie didn't know if Ahab understood. She didn't care. She just wanted to lead him away from the others. Azura was still breathing, steam escaped her lips and nose, even though her face was beaten to a pulp. Cassie couldn't tell if Darwin was breathing. Officer Richardson was either dead or unconscious.

"You remember me, don't you?" Cassie snarled between gritted teeth. "I took your eye."

Cassie gestured to her eye; the same one she took from Ahab. Surprisingly, the creature mimicked the gesture, raising a wrinkly paw to its face and touching the area just below his missing eye. Cassie thought she saw a look of sudden recognition on the creature's face.

"That's right. Come on ..."

Cassie bolted into the orchard. With a series of *whoops* and cries, Ahab gave chase. As Cassie sprinted into the darkness and fog that had completely enveloped the fruit trees, she moved by memory. She and Morgan had made this trip thousands of times. Tens of thousands, maybe. She shifted left, then right, then curved around. She could hear Ahab behind, five feet away at most. She could smell him. That familiar scent of mossy-mildew that suffused the air.

"Come on!" she screamed, desperate to keep the creature after her. Pushing herself harder, she put more distance between her and Ahab, who she hoped was tiring from the chase. He was on his hind legs, but his awkward limbs kept him hunched over as he ran. Cassie imagined the extra weight of those arms had to be exhausting.

Her lungs burned. Her sides ached. Her legs pistoned hard and she felt the beginnings of charley horses in her calves. But she kept running. Her breath came in sharp punches of steam that pushed from her nostrils and mouth and her mind spiraled back to the countless times she raced Morgan through the orchard. They were always headed to the same place. The place their parents warned them to stay away from.

The Pit.

Cassie exploded from the fruit trees and pushed herself harder. Once on the ledge of The Pit, she launched forward. She remembered the first time she tried jumping The Pit. Morgan had just left for basic training and she was lonely. Depressed. She almost didn't make it. She slammed hard against the incline on the opposite side and began slipping downward toward a broken window that had been deposited there before Cassie's family bought the orchard. Flecked with brown and yellow, the glass was largely intact at the time. Cassie imagined slipping into it, her legs getting torn apart in the process, but that never happened. She scrambled up the hill to safety, then walked the perimeter of The Pit back toward the guest house.

Tonight had to be different. The rush of wind in her face, Cassie prayed to whatever God was listening that she'd make it cleanly across. *Pleaseohpleaseohpleaseohplease* ...

When her Airwalks landed firmly on the ground, just beyond the mouth of The Pit, she steadied herself and turned quickly, just in time to see Ahab break through the orchard. He had an angry look on his face and the black hole that once held his other glowing gold eye stared back at her, a void Cassie thought she could fall into if she wasn't careful.

She didn't break eye contact. She wanted Ahab's eyes locked on her. Anywhere but its surroundings. Anywhere but the ground in front of him. Anywhere but The Pit. He charged, *whooping* and snarling, drool oozing from his open mouth, thick plumes of steam escaping from his gaping maw.

"Come get me!" Cassie screamed as Ahab neared the ledge.

🦍🦍🦍

The day after Cassie's bus incident, she found herself in gym class with Rose nearby, making comments under her breath. Cassie turned to her and scowled, which Rose took as a challenge.

"You got a problem?" Rose asked, turning toward Cassie.

"Maybe," Cassie said softly. "Fat little piggy."

Their classmates *oooh*'d at Cassie's retort. No one had stood up to Rose Balchi like that before. Not a single person. Rose pushed a smaller student out of the way and walked over to Cassie, standing nearly half a foot over her.

"Say that to my face," Rose said, her bulbous nose close to Cassie's.

"You. Are. A. Fat. Little. Piggy," Cassie said, emphasizing each word.

In a flash, Cassie raised her left hand to slap Rose in the face. *A feint.* As Rose easily recoiled from the left, she never saw Cassie's right. But instead of a slap, Cassie kept her hand tight in a fist. She caught Rose square on the chin, and the force of her attempting to duck the fake-left slap only added momentum to Cassie's right swing.

Rose fell to the mat of the gym, unconscious.

Cassie received both out-of-school and in-school suspension for the incident. Rose transferred to a school for kids with behavioral problems. From that day forward, nobody screwed with Cassie Albero. Her reputation had somehow matched Morgan's, who people knew to be a bit of a troublemaker but was never violent. Cassie, however, people knew not to mess with.

Each day in suspension, Cassie had to write about the experience. Never once did she apologize for it. Bernardo was disappointed, but Krystal understood. Morgan was downright proud, knowing that *sometimes you need to take matters into your own hands.*

And Cassie wrote that. Over and over. Different versions, but largely the same message. She didn't feel bad about what she did. Rose was a bully. She needed to be taught a lesson. If Cassie hadn't done it, somebody else might have. She didn't mean to knock her out.

But she was proud she did.

She felt the same sense of pride watching Ahab stumble over the edge of The Pit. His remaining eye went wide, realizing his mistake and loss of footing. The brightness of the gold told Cassie everything she needed to know. He was scared. *The key is to keep your eyes on the other guy's eyes.* Morgan's words echoed in Cassie's mind.

Cassie had heard things break before. Countless times. Hell, only hours earlier, windows on their home had been shattered under a hail of rocks from these creatures. But there were plenty of times when she and Morgan would throw rocks, broken toys, pieces of rebar, whatever they could find into The Pit to see it break the glass and other jagged, sharp nastiness that lay at the bottom.

The sound Ahab made as rusty pieces of mechanical equipment and shattered glass shredded his thick hide was horrific. Cassie watched the creature twist and snarl, screaming and tearing his skin and muscles to ribbons. Cassie imagined Big Red would've handled this differently. He probably would've been smart enough to avoid falling into The Pit, but not Ahab. Young, awkward Ahab. One-eyed and stupid, driven by instinct and rage. He was always going to fall.

He twisted, enormous shards of glass digging into his leathery black flesh, stretching and tearing his skin open. His leg was impaled on a piece of old tractor. His right hand was broken, the fingers bent at impossible angles. His one good eye blinked rapidly as blood misted from his mouth. As much as Ahab struggled, he couldn't get his leg loose of the tractor's broken, rusted exhaust pipe.

Cassie looked around for a rock large enough to finish the job. She remembered the farmers in town would talk about having to *put down* their livestock when an animal was injured and there was no possibility of recovery. Horses with broken legs. Cows dying from disease. Cassie saw Ahab as an animal and, as much as she loved watching it suffer for all that had happened, putting it down for good would be an act of mercy.

She found a few slabs of rock that might do the trick and used every last bit of strength to hoist one of them above her head. She stared down at Ahab, blood gurgling from its mouth, its fangs snapping wildly, biting the air itself, desperately gulping mouthfuls of oxygen as if it would somehow heal him.

Cassie thought of the past couple of months. The invasion of their property. The terror. The worry. The stress. She thought of her mom. *Jesus, where's my mom?* She imagined her mom being dragged into the woods. The creatures moved so quickly; she didn't see what happened. "Mom ..." she whimpered, before letting the slab of rock drop to the ground beside her.

Anger boiled in Cassie and she stared down at Ahab. He was frothing at the mouth, white foamy saliva bubbling and mingling with blood, forming a pinkish fluid that poured endlessly from his gaping maw. Filled with hate, Cassie reared back, remembering Azura standing over Old Gray. With a quick lean forward, Cassie spit directly into Ahab's good eye.

"This is your fault," Cassie said, turning away. She smelled it before she saw, acrid like dirty laundry.

Standing directly behind her was Mama. Yellow eyes glinting in the darkness and fog. Cassie tried to look away but couldn't. She was transfixed. The creature lumbered toward her slowly, hands outstretched. *Come to me*, Cassie imagined the creature saying. Instead, she only heard Ahab's ragged breathing and fruitless movement at the bottom of The Pit.

The stench filled Cassie's nostrils as Mama loomed tall above her. With a gracefulness Cassie hadn't previously witnessed, the female creature sidestepped Cassie and strode carefully to the edge of The Pit. It knelt slowly and reached downward. Cassie could barely move. Her hands twitched and her knees shook, wanting to break free of her reverie. But she couldn't. It was as if she was rooted in place, connected to the dirt through a force unknown.

Over her shoulder, she could just barely make out Mama pulling Ahab from The Pit. He squealed like a dying pig, grumbling and gurgling on his own bile and saliva. Slowly, Mama stepped past Cassie and finally, she saw Ahab slung over the larger creature's shoulder. His one good eye fell on Cassie, and he snarled with pure hate on his face.

Mama turned and looked at Cassie. For a moment, their eyes locked and Cassie believed she saw a humanity there. If only for an instant. Maybe they *were* closer to human than ape. That maybe Adriel was right and there was something spiritual about them. Something deeper. Something science and reality couldn't make heads or tails of.

When Mama's foot collided with Cassie's chest, all thoughts of commiseration escaped Cassie's mind. All she felt was searing pain radiating from the center of her chest outward. The *crack* that accompanied the kick let Cassie know that something immediately splintered under the force of the creature's big foot. She flew five feet sideways, landing hard along the edge of The Pit.

Mama carried Ahab into the forest, the gloom enveloping them. She was unable to move, and after a few minutes, the fog seemed to lift. Cassie fought for breath and listened for any sound of the creatures.

As she lay, chest heaving, in the dirt and stared at the star-filled sky. Thoughts of what waited for her on the other side flooded her mind and she felt scared. Not scared because she was going to die. Not that at all. Scared about how her dad would react. Scared for Morgan. Scared for their future. With her mother gone and with Cassie laying in the dirt, unable to breathe, she knew death wasn't far off.

"Daddy ... Morgan ..." Cassie gasped, her breath steaming into the night sky where the moon hung, glowing.

A blurry, almost liquid dark creeped into the girl's vision and the world began to fade to black.

CHAPTER THIRTEEN

Cassie awoke in the whitest room she'd ever seen. People in surgical masks moved around her and an enormous white light hung where the moon was only moments ago. *Was it moments? Where am I?*

"She's awake," one of the masked figures said.

"Jesus, put her out," another shouted.

In seconds, the world grew blurry and Cassie lost consciousness.

⸭ ⸭ ⸭

When Cassie's eyes opened again, she was lying flat on her back in a hospital room. There was a curtain to her right, obscuring the window, and at the foot of the bed were Bernardo and

Adriel. Adriel looked tired and was still wearing his clothing from the night before. *What time is it?* Cassie thought, her mind a cloud of confusion.

She looked to her left and saw Azura, a breathing tube in her mouth, her face heavily bandaged, but swollen lumps of purple-gray flesh were visible beneath what the bandages didn't cover. Cassie heard the *beep-beep-beep* of the equipment monitoring Azura's heart, then turned her head to see the equipment monitoring her own.

"Dad?"

Bernardo raised his head and looked at Cassie. There were tears in his eyes and he directed his gaze to the floor. To the window. He looked nervous, as though he had something to tell her.

"*Cucciola*," he said, stepping over to Cassie and taking her hand. "I'm so sorry, little one."

"What happened?" Cassie asked, her voice weak.

Adriel stepped forward. "All of your ribs, your sternum ... they're broken," he said. "You have a collapsed lung that the doctors had to repair. They said you woke up during the surgery."

"Surgery?" Cassie asked. She then turned to Bernardo. "Where's mom?"

Cassie had seen her dad cry before. But never like this. There was anger on his face. Frustration. It mingled with the sadness and the red puffiness around his eyes. He'd been crying all night.

Cassie felt a pang of guilt for bringing the tears on again. "I don't know, Cassandra. We couldn't find her."

Cassie looked around the room. "Where's Darwin?"

Adriel stepped closer and took Cassie's hand. "Just rest, okay?"

Cassie stared at the old man, confused. She wasn't stupid. She knew why he was telling her to rest. There was something he didn't want to tell her. Something he didn't think she could handle. He didn't know what happened at The Pit. He didn't know that Cassie was capable of just about anything. She could *handle* just about anything. But maybe that wasn't true. Maybe Cassie was just angry at being kept in the dark. She felt heat in her chest, and she wondered about the surgery. Her lung. She wondered what happened to Ahab.

She hoped he was dead.

🦍 🦍 🦍

After being discharged from the hospital, Cassie sat in the El Camino with her ChatBoy, playing the sounds from the night the creatures attacked. The *whoops*, roars, and other terrifying noises didn't frighten her anymore, and she thought about all the things she learned since getting out of the hospital.

Darwin had disappeared. More likely, the boy was taken in like her mom. Cassie didn't understand. She tried her best not to think about why the creatures would want two humans. Inevitably, the thought of her mom being gone made her cry and the thought of something horrifying being *done* to her mother made her angry. Darwin was weak. Gangly. Awkward in the way Ahab was awkward. *What good was he to them*? Cassie would often think.

September rolled around and school started, but Cassie wasn't healed enough to go back. Bernardo had taken it upon himself to teach her, with Adriel's help. With Krystal gone, Bernardo couldn't keep up the orchard and so he sold it to Adriel, who offered a fair price, though Cassie knew her dad was heartbroken to see it all go. She also knew he was happy to leave a place that held so many horrible memories.

Cassie often thought about how cruel one summer could be. How one summer could change so much for so many people. Mom gone. Darwin gone. Azura in a coma, her face ripped to shreds and smashed apart. Officer Richardson dead.

That last bit was the most difficult part. Cassie watched her dad speak to the police, both from Lakeside and Resting Hollow, about the death of an off-duty officer on orchard property. Adriel had coached Bernardo in what to say. They were hunting. There had been a bear problem in recent months. A big one broke the property line and attacked.

The Resting Hollow police made a big deal about Azura and Darwin being there illegally and made mention that once Azura woke up, she'd be sent back to El Salvador by immigration officials. The thought of Azura waking up to news that her son was missing and that she was being forced back to her home country made Cassie sick to her stomach.

In many ways, she prayed Azura never woke up because maybe in the woman's dreams, she was still with her son.

Home-schooling with Bernardo in their new abode above Adriel's shop wasn't the same as regular school. Cassie felt strange not being able to see her few friends. Morgan was on his way home, though, having returned to Saudi Arabia by mid-September and finally learning about Krystal having gone missing.

Once home, he wanted to squeeze Cassie tight, but held back, knowing she was still on the mend. She watched as her brother hugged their dad a long time, still in his cammies. Almost immediately, Morgan began to cry.

That night at dinner, they ate in silence. Bernardo continued to set a place for Krystal and Cassie wondered why. Her dad had changed. Where there had once been a lightness in him, now there was nothing more than weight. Cassie heard him crying every night from her bedroom. Bernardo slept each night on the couch, often with the television blaring, and Cassie knew he stayed up late waiting for Krystal to come home. Waiting for something. Any news. Any information about where she was.

Krystal never appeared.

Morgan took Cassie for a drive in the El Camino and listened to the recording. He didn't understand at first, but knew his sister and father weren't liars, so once the absurdity of the situation faded from his mind, he knew that the truth was far more insidious than he imagined. Some monster had taken his mother. Some monster had taken a little boy. Some monster had killed a police officer. Some monster had cost his family everything.

Morgan was angry. They sometimes walked the foothills together and Morgan would stare into the deep woods, rifle slung over his shoulder. Cassie knew he was waiting for something to appear.

Nothing ever appeared.

"What's an honorable discharge?" Cassie asked on one such walk in the woods near their old home.

"It means that I've done my duty and am done being a Marine, I guess," Morgan said, stepping over a large crop of roots from an enormous elm. "But you're never *really* done being a Marine, kiddo."

There were times when Cassie would awaken late at night and find Bernardo asleep on the couch, but Morgan nowhere to be found. She knew he was in the woods, alone, looking for their mother. He had started working for Adriel and used every scrap of money he made to buy guns. Ammo. Whatever he believed would help. Cassie worried about her brother. She worried about her father. Most of the time, she just *worried*.

Eventually, Cassie returned to school. A year had gone by and she missed being with the other kids. Rumors circulated that something happened at the Albero Orchard, and even though kids asked her about it constantly, Cassie ignored them. They'd want to know if her dad was a murderer. If her mom was taken by goblins from the mountains. If her brother had gone crazy. The usual cruel, childish absurdity. Cassie knew the truth. So did Bernardo and Adriel. Even Morgan.

Cassie visited Azura every week, bringing fresh flowers she grew in their garden window box. The tiny bouquet brought some much needed color to the room and as Cassie told Azura about her day at school, about Morgan's job and about her dad crying every night, she hoped Azura could hear her. On more than one occasion, Cassie helped the nurses shift Azura in bed and didn't ask about things like bed sores or blood clots or anything like that. Cassie had seen and learned enough the previous summer to last a lifetime.

Jellybean remained by Cassie's side, growing older, slowing down the way dogs do. His recovery was nothing short of a miracle, according to Bernardo. The Labrador was tough. Brave. Only when Cassie went to school would Jellybean leave her, waiting near the front door of the apartment for her return each afternoon.

As Cassie grew older, she would drive her brother's El Camino down to the orchard, which sat empty and overgrown. There was talk the county was going to develop the land into condominiums or apartments, but those plans never materialized. The land was Adriel's now, and Cassie didn't really care much.

But she found herself walking The Pit and, over time, the exact area where Ahab had fallen started to evaporate from her mind.

She'd stare down at the broken, jagged pieces of metal and glass and remember Ahab dying below her. She realized, thanks to her therapist, that she felt powerful in that moment. She controlled another creature's life. Even though she didn't kill Ahab herself, she hoped his injuries got the better of him. She never felt remorse for that hope, even though her shrink preached the virtues of forgiveness and moving on and all that headshrinker nonsense that Cassie knew was helpful to a point.

But not with monsters who steal your mother. Not with monsters who take little boys into the woods.

As Cassie stood along the edge of The Pit, she heard birdsong in the distance. The buzzing of flies in the orchard, still eating whatever fruit the trees produced. She turned to the forest and stared into it. The thick, verdant leaves waved to her, beckoning Cassie to enter.

The woods called to her. They always had. Even as a little girl, she felt at home there and she thought about exploring with Darwin years earlier. Telling him how comfortable she felt among the trees. There was never fear. Just curiosity. Cassie wasn't a hunter. She had no desire to seek out elk or boar or other game animals. Cassie felt alive in the woods. Maybe that's how Morgan felt on his nocturnal escapades.

Her eyes on the woods, she thought she saw two flickering gold eyes stare back at her. But they were gone just as fast as they appeared. They may never have been there at all. Cassie hadn't seen the eyes in years, so she thought that maybe it was all in her head. She took a tentative step toward the forest. The breeze tousled her hair and Jellybean rubbed against her legs. She knelt and ran her hands across the dog's haunches, then behind his ears.

Then she walked.

Slowly.

Carefully.

With Jellybean by her side, stepping through the overgrown roots and mossy rocks, Cassie walked into the forest.

A thick fog and the absence of all woodland sound greeted them.

THE END

QUICK Favor

Thank you so much for dedicating your time to reading this book! May we ask a quick favor?

Will you please take a moment to leave a review on Amazon, Goodreads, or wherever you purchased the book? Your words have power. Your review can help this book reach more readers. We appreciate you!

About the Author

Robert P. Ottone is the Bram Stoker Award-winning author of THE TRIANGLE and is also the best-selling author of CURSE OF THE COB MAN, THE SLEEPY HOLLOW GANG, THE VILE THING WE CREATED and NOCTURNAL CREATURES.

His short fiction has been collected in WRAPPED IN PLASTIC AND OTHER SWEET NOTHINGS as well as HER INFERNAL NAME & OTHER NIGHTMARES.

He holds two master's degrees in Education, as well as an MFA in Children's Literature.

A bagel-loving fabulist of spooky absurdity, Ottone enjoys cigars, cocktails and time with his wife.

www.ingramcontent.com/pod-product-compliance
Lightning Source LLC
Chambersburg PA
CBHW061349310726
48974CB00001B/260